The Writer's Wife

Is Anything Real?

GLEN EBISCH

The Writer's Wife

Glen Ebisch

Published by Glen Ebisch, 2022.

This is a work of fiction. Similarities to real people, places, or events are entirely coincidental.

THE WRITER'S WIFE

First edition. September 3, 2022.

Copyright © 2022 Glen Ebisch.

Written by Glen Ebisch.

Table of Contents

For Robert B. Atkin with friendship and respect.

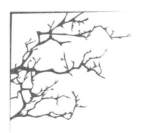

Chapter One

I will always remember when we heard about the death of Harrison Cole.

We were sitting in the living room of our cottage. Jonathan was in his usual easy chair in front of the television, while I was on the sofa off to the side, craning my neck to see the screen. He had his writing board on his lap and was making his way through a pile of student papers. He had the usual intent expression on his face that he got when grading student writing. They must not have been very good because he was sighing even more frequently than usual, and the red pen was flying over the pages.

I was glancing over my teaching notes for the next day. I taught history at the local public high school, and although I made out careful lesson plans for each day and had a well-designed outline of the material, I always liked to take a quick glance over the next day's lessons to make sure I didn't forget any of the points I wanted to make. My name is Sarah McAdams, originally Sarah Lane, until I married Jonathan a little over ten years ago.

I was half reading my notes and half watching television when the anchor for the national evening news announced at almost the end of the broadcast that Harrison Cole had died after suffering a fall in his home. A brief summary of his life and works followed. Although I rarely read anything other than historical fiction and lumped thrillers in the same category as horror, both fields I avoided, even I recognized the name of Harrison Cole as being in the same league as Stephen King and James Patterson, two other authors I was also aware of but never considered reading.

"Did you see that?" I said to Jonathan. "Harrison Cole has died."

Jonathan glanced up with a bewildered smile on his face. I have always admired his ability to concentrate. While I find it difficult to work in front of the television, my attention quickly drifting to whatever was being discussed on the screen, Jonathan, when grading papers or reading a book, can tune out all distractions and go into a world of his own.

"What did you say?" he asked with a vague smile.

"Harrison Cole died. He fell in his home."

Jonathan nodded slowly. "The death of another literary hack. Although every man's death diminishes me, his doesn't do so very much."

"Still, he was a very popular writer," I replied.

"Popularity is no proof of merit."

I let the comment go, not wanting to get Jonathan up on his hobbyhorse about the difference between literature and commercial fiction. I was relieved when Jonathan returned to his papers instead of launching into another of his lectures on how debased modern culture has become. He could be very funny and even eloquent on the topic, but I'd heard it all before and could almost recite it verbatim.

I knew that much of what he said was based on opinions he'd gotten from his English professors in college. They said that true literature provided new insights into life and the world, while commercial fiction was simply entertainment. The difference between nourishment and junk food, as Jonathan liked to say. And just as modern culture encouraged unhealthy eating, it also promoted unhealthy reading, leaving the average person's mind ill-nourished.

Although I knew that Jonathan had a point and certainly lived according to his beliefs, reading works by obscure Nobel Prize winners from eastern Europe and Booker Prize finalists with only a small following, while remaining completely oblivious to those authors on *The New York Times* bestseller list, I'd found myself wondering recently how much of his attitude was based on envy rather than on carefully formulated ideas.

I'd met Jonathan in college in the one creative writing class I had taken, at a time when I'd briefly toyed in a dreamy way with the idea of writing as a career. He had been the star of the creative writing program, having already had a couple of short stories published in distinguished literary journals, and when we married right after graduation, I had taken a teaching position with the shared understanding that I would support him until he became a successful writer. After that happened, we thought we'd be free to pursue life in whatever way we wanted. The opportunities at the time seemed boundless.

Several more short stories had been published over the following three years, but the novel Jonathan had worked on steadily for the five years after that still showed no sign of being accepted by an agent, many of whom praised his writing but said they would have no chance of selling it to a publisher in the current market. By the time we'd reached our early thirties, I was tenured and had become reconciled to the idea that teaching was my future. Although I enjoyed teaching and found it rewarding, I had to admit on occasion to harboring feelings of regret that life hadn't worked out exactly as we had planned.

When the repeated rejections had come in for his novel, Jonathan's anger and despair had deepened until I'd begun to worry. Attempting to salvage his mental health, I suggested that he might get a Master of Fine Arts in writing and attempt to find a position teaching creative writing in a local college. Although reluctant to give up full-time writing, he had eventually agreed.

Again, he had excelled in the program, and after graduating, he had gotten a couple of temporary teaching positions. But they never seemed to last long. Jonathan claimed it was because he wouldn't compromise his standards, and he gave me withering looks when I suggested that you had to meet students where they were rather than expecting them to rise to your level. He currently was an adjunct, teaching two writing courses, at a local community college, and although knowing that my advice wouldn't be appreciated, I kept making gentle suggestions that he might want to be more accommodating with his students than in the past in the hope that this might lead to a permanent position.

In my heart, I knew that he would be happier if he had a full-time job that conferred some sense of dignity. It wouldn't be the same as being a published novelist, but it would be more than he had now. But I approached the topic warily because, although generally even tempered, anything that suggested he was a failure as a writer was sure to lead to an impressive fit of anger.

"I seem to remember an article in the local paper about Harrison Cole," I said, turning my attention back to the television. "Didn't he live near here. Somewhere down in the vicinity of Great Barrington."

"Did he?" Jonathan said, not looking up.

"Yes. I think they said he had a cottage in that area. Of course, it could be one of those nineteenth century rich folks' places that were called cottages but were really more like mansions."

"Hmm," Jonathan said, not really paying attention.

"We should go down there some time and take a tour of the historic homes. It's only about twenty miles south of here."

Even though we'd lived in the Berkshires of Massachusetts for over ten years and had moved from an apartment into our house over three years ago, we rarely traveled around the area. Whenever we did take a vacation, Jonathan wanted to go down to Manhattan for "a dose of culture" as he called it.

Jonathan tossed the pile of papers on the floor. "Enough of this for tonight. My brain needs reviving. I think I'll go up to my study and write for a while."

We had turned the second upstairs bedroom into a study for Jonathan where he had a desk, bookshelves, and his computer. I tended to float around the house with my laptop, working wherever there was room, preparing my lesson plans and sending out emails. Fiction writing required a quiet place to think and reflect, while my own efforts could be accomplished almost anywhere.

"How's the story going?" I asked, as he walked across the room.

He stopped and gave me a long look. "You know I don't like to talk about anything that I'm still working on. It tends to sap the creative energy."

I nodded. The fact that he had said the words gently and not snapped them out like a machine gun indicated that things must be going well. He had been working on a second novel for over six months, hoping this would prove more commercially viable than the first.

I breathed a quiet sigh of relief as he gave me one of his dazzling smiles. Although we were both over thirty, he was as good looking as he had been in college with his thick, dark, wavy hair and deep-set brown eyes. I still had to pinch myself sometimes to realize that he had chosen me above all the other young women who had been gaga about him in college. Even though I knew that I had been attractive then and still was, some of those women had been talented as well as beautiful. Whenever I asked him why he had chosen me, he would grin and ruffle my hair and say that it was because I was uniquely who I am.

"Well, I'm going upstairs to write because . . ." He paused in the doorway waiting for me.

I knew my cue. "That's what writers do. They write," I said, dutifully finishing his little nightly mantra.

He gave me a smile and a thumbs up, then left for his world of fiction.

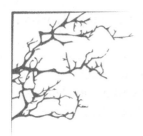

Chapter Two

The call came a week later.

Jonathan only had to go into the college three days a week, but it happened to be on one of his working days when the call came. He had gotten home a few minutes after me. I was in the kitchen preparing dinner when he strolled in asking what we were going to eat. Right after giving me a peck on the cheek, his cell phone rang. He glanced at the number with a puzzled expression and then reluctantly answered it.

"Hello."

I could tell that whatever the caller said immediately caught his attention. I stared at him, looking for some indication on his face as to whether it was bad news about someone in our family. But he seemed excited rather than alarmed, and my concern dissipated when I heard him say, "Yes, I think I've heard of those books."

Whoever was on the other end continued at some length. Finally, Jonathan said, "Yes. Meeting here next Tuesday afternoon would be fine, and I'll certainly give your offer serious consideration."

When he ended the call, he turned to face me. He appeared pale.

"Is everything all right?" I asked.

He nodded. "That was Lynn Samson, she's a literary agent in New York."

"And she wants to publish your novel," I said in delight.

"No such luck," Jonathan replied glumly. "But it isn't all bad. Apparently, Harrison Cole designated in his will that I should be given the first opportunity to audition to continue writing his Duke Danforth adventure series."

I shook my head, confused. "Why would Harrison Cole select you to continue his series?"

"Well, we met once," Jonathan said slowly.

"You met?" I said, not sure I'd heard him correctly. "You never told me that you'd met Harrison Cole, and you certainly didn't let on a week ago when I told you about his death."

Jonathan blushed. "Well, we weren't exactly the best of friends. It was at that Boston conference on writing the modern novel. He was on one of the panels that I attended. I happened to come down to breakfast early the next morning, and he was already at a table in the ballroom sitting by himself. He looked a bit lonely, so I went over and told him how much I'd enjoyed his presentation. You know I like talking to older people. You can learn a lot."

I had to admit that was true. Jonathan always seemed to enjoy talking with my father, which I found to be hard going.

"You must have made quite an impression on him for Cole to put you in his will."

"I suppose."

"I guess you didn't tell him that he was a literary hack."

Jonathan gave a small smile. "I'm not usually as blunt in person as I am when talking with you. Anyway, although I may not think what he wrote was literature, he did write very entertaining fiction."

"Have you read any of his books?"

He shook his head. "I've glanced at some reviews. But I guess I had better read one or two now, so I can tell Lynn Samson whether I want to take a shot at carrying on the Duke Danforth series."

"Are you actually considering it?" I asked in surprise. "I mean, it would be a 180-degree turn from the type of thing you've been working on all your life."

"I know it's unlikely that I'll want to do it, but Samson was very persuasive that I should at least listen to her pitch."

"Couldn't she have just given it over the phone? It must be inconvenient for her to travel all the way up here from New York City."

"Apparently, Cole's granddaughter must also approve the selection of the author to carry on his legacy. Cole's daughter and her husband are both dead, so she's his next of kin. She's living in a hotel down in Great Barrington while settling his estate. Samson is bringing her along to discuss matters with me."

"I suppose if you did take it on, you might become better known and make some real money."

"Yeah, I guess so."

"But you'd be writing books with a main character developed by another person, and it wouldn't be writing . . ."

"Literature. I know that." He paused and his face contorted. "It's just that I'm so tired of being a failure."

I went over and hugged him tight. "You're not a failure. Your talent just hasn't been recognized yet. But are you sure you want to give up on what you're doing just to carry on another man's work? We get along fine on what we earn from our teaching, and this way you can continue with your second novel."

He stepped back from me. "How long do we have until dinner?"

"About an hour."

He nodded. "I think I'll run into town to the bookstore and see whether I can pick up any books in the Duke Danforth series."

As he hurried out the kitchen door, I wondered if he had already made up his mind.

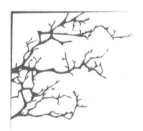

Chapter Three

A week later, I was sitting in the living room when the knock came at the door. Jonathan was upstairs in his study poring over the two Duke Danforth novels he'd been able to purchase locally. He'd been reading them in the detailed way he did when studying great literature, writing extensive notes in the margins and analyzing their style and structure. I waited for him to answer the door—he certainly knew who it must be; after all, we had been aware of the impending visit for a week—but when there was a second knock and no sign that he was coming down the stairs, I sighed and walked out into the hall.

Two women stood on the front porch. The one nearest to me was a woman in her fifties, wearing a loose blouse and a full skirt that hung from her sizable hips almost to the ground. Her salt and pepper hair flew in wild disarray, as if she had just walked through a high wind even though it was a calm early October day. Next to her was a slender woman in her midtwenties, looking both beautiful and stylish in a pencil skirt and scoop-necked blouse covered by a linen jacket. Her long, brown hair gave her a girlish look that contrasted with her professional dress. The older woman stuck out her hand and gave a surprisingly warm smile.

"I assume that you're the writer's wife?" she asked "I'm Lynn Samson. I spoke with your husband a week ago."

"Of course," I replied. A little flustered, I gave the hand a timid shake.

"And this is Amanda Beaumont, Harrison Cole's granddaughter."

A slender white hand was tentatively extended and briefly touched mine.

"Won't you come in? My husband will be right down."

As they came into the short hall that led to the living room, I became aware that Jonathan was standing in stillness at the top of the stairs, like an actor waiting for the right moment to make his entrance onstage.

"Hello, everyone," he said in a hearty voice, rushing noisily down the uncarpeted stairs as if surprised to see them.

The introductions were performed again and then everyone went into the living room. The two visitors sat on the sofa, while Jonathan took his usual spot across from them. I found myself relegated to a straight-backed, wooden chair off to the side. There were several moments of idle conversation about the trip, whether there had been any difficulty finding the house, and formal condolences were extended to Amanda on her grandfather's death.

"Would anyone like some tea or coffee?" I asked.

"Perhaps after we've discussed our business," Lynn said in a firm tone. She suddenly clapped her hands together as if to get the attention of a large, noisy crowd. "So, Jonathan, you've had time to consider our proposition and no doubt taken the opportunity to acquaint yourself with the Duke Danforth novels. Would you like to take a try at becoming the next Harrison Cole?"

"Well, as you can imagine, it would be quite an about-face for me since all my previous writing has been more literary in nature," he began in his professor voice.

"Yes. I've examined your resume online," Samson said in a neutral tone, which still managed to suggest that she wasn't about to be flummoxed by any efforts to inflate the minimal success of his literary career so far.

Jonathan paused, slightly taken aback. "After considerable discussion with my wife, I've come to the conclusion that I would like to give it a try."

I twitched on my hard chair. It was true that we had talked about the matter sporadically but hardly at length or in any great depth. Jonathan had seemed reluctant to examine the issue. Whenever I tried to get him to systematically consider the pros and cons of both sides, Jonathan impatiently said that he was mulling it over in his own time and didn't want to beat it to death. That wasn't surprising. I've always had the more analytical mind about everything but literature. When it comes to life, Jonathan tends to rely on intuition and the "truths of the subconscious," as he calls them, for giving him guidance.

Lynn Samson nodded. "Yes. It's always helpful to discuss big life decisions with someone," she said, giving me a lingering look. "As I told you over the phone, we'd like you to write a few chapters of what you see the next Danforth novel as being, and then Amanda and I will evaluate it to see if it seems to be in the style and spirit of Harrison's work."

"Wouldn't Cole's publisher also have a say in that decision?" I asked, earning myself an annoyed glance from Jonathan.

"Of course, ultimately his editor will have the final say, but she's worked with Cole and me for many years and would very likely accept a decision arrived at by Amanda and myself. The Danforth novels are a cash cow, so they're motivated to have them keep coming in a timely way."

I continued my questioning. "Will people continue to buy the Danforth novels if they know that the original author is dead?" This seemed to me to be the type of important business question that Jonathan should be asking.

"Hard to tell," Lynn admitted. "There have been several successful series in the past few years that have done very well when continued by a new author. The important thing is to come as close to sounding like the original as possible."

"So imitation is the byword?" I asked, glancing over at my husband to see if he seemed disturbed by the thought of essentially copying another man's work. But he sat there with an inscrutable expression on his face.

Lynn smiled. "Well, you can't break the mold, only crack it a little around the edges. And the first

couple of novels at least should adhere strictly to the
style of those that have gone before."

"Is there anything else Jonathan should know?" I
asked.

"The publisher wants to get the next Danforth
book out quickly. The last one came out in the stores
four weeks ago, and it has done very well. The next
must be available on the market in a year's time, so it
should already have been completed and submitted by
now. Going through the publishing pipeline takes at
least a year." Lynn turned to Jonathan. "So, you'll
have to write like the wind."

"Did Harrison leave any notes for his next
novel?" Jonathan asked, breaking his silence.

"Not that we've been able to find," Lynn replied.
"Amanda thoroughly searched his study without
success."

"Do you know why my grandfather selected you
to carry on his work?" Amanda suddenly said,
looking hard at Jonathan. She had a lilting, almost
musical, voice that would draw attention in any
crowd.

Jonathan gave her one of his winning smiles. "We
met at a conference several years ago and had a long,
friendly conversation."

"Did the two of you keep in touch after that
time?" Amanda asked.

"No. I felt funny about bothering an important
man like that. I thought it would appear as if I were
angling for something. And I certainly never expected
him to contact me." Jonathan gave a self-deprecating
laugh. "After all, I'm sure he met lots of young

writers at conferences. He could hardly be expected to keep track of them all."

"Yet, he did remember you," she persisted.

"Apparently so."

"Okay, then," Lynn Samson interrupted, getting the conversation back on track. "We're agreed that you will write within the next month—let's say—the first twenty-five thousand words of what you see as becoming the next Duke Danforth novel. Amanda and I will evaluate your efforts and arrive at a decision regarding whether you are given a contract to become the next Harrison Cole."

"Will Jonathan's name be on the cover as the author?" I asked.

"Oh, yes. He's the new writer of the Danforth novels, not a ghostwriter. He'll get full credit."

"What would the compensation be?" I said, glancing at Jonathan and wondering why he had become mute.

Lynn frowned. "Let's not put the cart before the horse. We can always discuss financial matters once Jonathan has been selected to write the novels."

"When I was a little girl, I would often visit my grandfather at the cottage. He'd let me play in his study while he was writing. I've always had fond memories of those times," Amanda said in a dreamy tone. "I was wondering whether you could show me your study. It might help me to decide if you have the right personality to carry on my grandfather's legacy."

Jonathan looked nonplussed for a moment, then he smiled. "I'm afraid my study isn't very prepossessing, but you are certainly welcome to see it."

"I'd like that." Amanda stood in one graceful move and turned toward me. "Perhaps we could now have that tea you offered."

"Of course," I said, feeling very much ordered around, although the girl had not exactly been rude. I headed out into the kitchen to prepare things, briefly watching Jonathan pause to allow Amanda to go up the stairs first.

A few minutes later, as I was arranging items on a tray, Lynn Samson came into the kitchen. The woman walked across the room and stared out the back window.

"Is all that land yours?" she asked.

"The house is on two acres, most of it in the back. That's one of the reasons why we chose it. Beyond our property line is pastureland that no one uses. All the houses on this side of the road have lots of privacy."

"And you can see all the way to the hills beyond. They look particularly colorful this time of year."

"The fall is special, but every season of the year has its own beauty."

"Sometimes I think for a moment I should leave the city and move to a place like this. After all, literary agents can work from anywhere today what with everything being done via the internet."

"Wouldn't you miss the excitement of urban life?" I asked, pouring the hot water into the tea pot.

Lynn gave a throaty chuckle. "Of course I would. That's why the desire quickly passes. The quiet of the countryside would drive me crazy in a week. At night

I'd miss the sounds of the sirens telling me that there were still other people alive in the world. And if I didn't hear the old fellow in the apartment next to mine coughing up a lung every morning, how would I know when to get up."

I laughed. "I suppose there's something to be said for city life, but I prefer a quieter existence."

"Savor it," Lynn said curtly. "If your husband gets this deal, your quiet days will be over."

"How do you mean?"

"Oh, it's not like being a recognizable movie star with paparazzi following you everywhere. But he'll suddenly be in demand to go to conferences, be on panels, and give presentations. Magazines will want him to write small pieces for them, and he'll start hearing from an army of fans, most of them women. But the worst will be the pressure to wash, rinse, and repeat."

I gave her a puzzled glance.

"If the first book is a success, he'll be expected to do it all over again within less than a year."

"Jonathan is a very disciplined writer," I said a shade defensively.

Lynn waved a dismissive hand. "Anyone can produce when their stuff isn't being read by anyone other than family and friends. The problem arises when you're famous and expected to top your last novel with the next. The pressure can be immense. That's why there are so many one-hit wonders in the literary world. It's not that they don't have the talent to write another fine novel, but the expectation to do so messes with their heads."

"But some writers manage."

"Usually, it's because they have a supportive home life that keeps them grounded. Even an old warhorse like Harrison Cole, who'd been at it for thirty years, began to struggle three years ago when his wife died. Granted, he was already in his seventies, but he'd been doing his novel a year with no problem up until then. Once Grace passed away, however, he seemed to be foundering. It took him over two years to get out his next book. If he'd been a new guy without a great track record, his publisher might have dropped him. As it was, I had to run interference for Harrison with everyone from his editor to the head of the fiction department. Of course, they were getting pressure from upstairs. Everything in the business today is run by bean counters sitting back in the main office of some international conglomerate that has nothing to do with publishing."

"So, you're saying that if Jonathan gets this contract, it will put more pressure on me to support him?"

"What I'm saying is that it will be your full-time job."

"I've already got a position that I like in teaching."

Lynn reached out and touched my shoulder, giving me a sympathetic glance.

"Then get ready, sweetheart, because you're about to have two full-time jobs."

"DO YOU THINK THIS IS going to work out?" I asked, after Lynn and Amanda had left.

"Why shouldn't it?" Jonathan said with a grin. "I don't think I'll have any trouble imitating the old boy's style. He wasn't exactly James Joyce."

"But what about coming up with twisty plots? Isn't that the whole point of a thriller, to surprise the reader at the last moment?"

"It's pretty much a formula, honey. You just read a couple of them, and you've got it down."

I sighed and took the dirty dishes out to the kitchen. A few minutes later, Jonathan followed me.

"What's bothering you?" he asked. "You're awfully quiet. I thought you'd be pleased that I finally have an opportunity to be published."

I turned, draped my arm around his waist, and gave him a gentle squeeze. "I am happy for you, but I just worry that this isn't going to be fulfilling for you because it's not the kind of literary success that you've always dreamed about."

"There's nothing saying that eventually I can't do both. After all, I can always write serious fiction under a pen name while I continue writing the Harrison Cole novels. Some literary writers do popular fiction under a pseudonym."

I nodded doubtfully. That sounded to me like one of those good ideas that was never going to happen.

Jonathan frowned. "Look, this is my entrance into the fraternity of writers. Once I can show myself able to do steady work as a published author, all sorts of other things will open up for me. Publishers will know my name and take anything I write seriously."

I nodded, dismissing my reservations as being silly because after all, Jonathan knew a lot more about the world of writing than I did. And whereas in the past, he could hardly get an agent to respond to his queries, today we'd had a famous one sitting right in our living room. That had to be a sign of good things to come. I turned and gave Jonathan an enthusiastic hug.

"That's my girl," he said. "How about we go out to dinner tonight to celebrate?"

I hesitated momentarily and watched the sulky expression return to his face.

"We've got to live for the moment, Sarah. We can't always be worrying about the future. This is a time to dance on the table."

I smiled. "I understand that, but I'd be more comfortable if we waited to celebrate until you've signed a contract. Then I promise, I'll go out and dance on the table right alongside you."

"Okay. But how about for tonight we at least open a bottle of sparkling wine."

"I'd say that sounds just about right."

That night after getting a little tipsy, we went to bed early and made love with the passion I remembered from the early years of our marriage when Jonathan still had great expectations for his first novel. More than anything, this made me hope that he was making the right decision in becoming the new Harrison Cole.

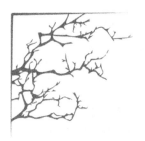

Chapter Four

Beginning the next night, Jonathan cut short the amount of time he spent grading student papers, and for the next week, he went up to his study early to write. I always wished him luck, but I was concerned that he was neglecting his teaching duties and would end up losing his position at the college. Try as I might, I couldn't find it within me to share Jonathan's confidence in his ability to write thrillers. Was it possible that he could successfully produce a type of novel that in his heart he despised? I knew too many teachers who were just going through the motions to get a paycheck to feel happy at the prospect of Jonathan doing something similar. Then I chided myself for being too negative. Jonathan loved to write, and wasn't there something similar about all forms of literature that would appeal to his creativity? And I had to admire his self-confidence because I truly believed that little was achieved in life without having a deep belief in one's own abilities.

These thoughts bounced around in my head for the next seven days until the following Friday when Jonathan announced, shortly before going to bed, that he had completed ten thousand words of the new manuscript.

"It's amazing that you've gotten that much written, especially with everything you have to do at school."

"Well, I may have cut a few corners there," Jonathan admitted sheepishly. "But you have to prioritize to get ahead."

"I suppose."

"I'll be showing what I've got done to Amanda tomorrow morning."

"Why?"

"She asked to see it, and I didn't think it would be diplomatic to refuse."

"Down at her hotel?"

"I guess. She hasn't moved into her grandfather's cottage yet. She's having it cleaned from top to bottom first. I guess her grandfather had let things slide over the last few years since his wife's death."

"Did you contact her that you'd completed ten thousand words?"

"Actually, she's been in touch with me just about every day giving me suggestions and wanting to see what I've got done." He rolled his eyes. "I've kind of put her off as long as I can."

"You certainly want to stay on her good side since she's one of the people with a say over whether you get a contract," I said. "But be careful to keep a professional distance."

I could easily visualize the cute little miss who had ordered me to provide tea while waltzing upstairs with my husband as having designs on Jonathan. Amanda was obviously someone who felt entitled and would try to take whatever she wanted, including Jonathan if he was on offer. I knew that there were a few men who truly did have eyes only for their wives, but I didn't number Jonathan among them. He was too attractive not to enjoy a bit of flirting.

"Of course I'll be professional," Jonathan said in a hurt tone, as if he were completely oblivious to other women. "And don't worry, I only need to keep her sweet until the first book is published. After that, I'll be on my own and can forget I ever met her."

THE NEXT MORNING, THE thought of Jonathan and Amanda sitting side-by-side together in a cozy hotel room was still on my mind as I washed up after breakfast. I hadn't mentioned the matter to Jonathan because I didn't want to sound like a nag, and I had read in a magazine that acting suspicious of your husband could encourage him to stray. Probably on the reasoning that if you're going to be suspected of something, you might as well do it. But it preyed on my mind, and I found myself checking the clock throughout the morning, wondering what was happening in that hotel room. I didn't like myself for being a suspicious wife, but I had pegged Amanda as a predatory woman, and Jonathan's sometimes overly emotional approach to life could easily make him a victim. And if he went down, so did our marriage.

It came as something of a relief to me when the front doorbell rang midmorning, providing me with a distraction. When I opened the door, our next-door neighbor, Maggie Boyd, was on the doorstep.

"Hi, Sarah, I'm taking a run down to the church recycling shop, and I wondered if you had anything to go. You usually do."

"Come into the living room for a moment, and I'll take a look."

Upstairs in our bedroom, I found a bag of my old sweaters and slacks ready to be given away. I'm a strong believer in not hanging on to things that I don't wear anymore. I seemed to remember that Jonathan had mentioned having a few shirts in a bag in the study closet that could also be given away, so I went into the room and found a white plastic bag in the back of his closet. When I checked, it contained a few shirts that I hadn't seen him wear in years. Even though Jonathan tended to be sentimental about clothes, keeping them because they reminded him of fun times, I was pretty sure that these were safe to donate. As I lifted the bag, I glanced down and saw that it had been covering a box of books. The top of the box was open, and I could easily see that those on top were all Harrison Cole novels. I wondered for a moment when he had purchased them since I had only been aware of the two he had bought in the bookstore in town. Putting the thought aside, I hurried downstairs.

"Here you go, Maggie," I said, dropping the bags at the end of the sofa where my neighbor sat. "Thanks for thinking of me."

"No problem. And congratulations on the exciting news."

I gave her a puzzled look.

"About Jonathan having the opportunity to become the next Harrison Cole. I hope you're both going to still talk to me once you're famous."

"He told you about that?" I asked, struggling to keep the annoyance out of my voice. Why was Jonathan being so foolish? Spreading the word around when he wasn't even certain that he'd get a contract just wasn't smart. I knew that he was bitter about being unrecognized as a writer for so long, but what if he didn't get the job, the embarrassment of having to tell everyone things were off would make the pain of rejection that much greater.

Maggie looked stricken. "Was I not supposed to know? It wasn't like I was prying or anything. I just happened to be in the front yard when Jonathan went off to work one morning last week, and he called me over and told me. He was obviously very excited about it."

"Yes. Jonathan does tend to get excited about things, and there's certainly nothing wrong with your knowing. But I'd appreciate it if you didn't spread it around because it isn't exactly a done deal yet."

Maggie reached over and touched the back of my hand. "Of course. It stops with me." She smiled. "Men can be such little boys sometimes, can't they? When life is going well, it's all Christmas presents and rainbows, but let a few waves come along and you'd think it was the end of the world."

I nodded. I didn't know Maggie very well. We chatted three or four times a month when we happened to run into each other. She was around forty, and I had heard from local scuttlebutt that her husband had left her five years ago for a younger model that he'd met at work. Fortunately, Maggie had in-demand IT skills that had allowed her to work from home while raising her two children. The boy was now around eight and the girl twelve, and Maggie often talked about how much she appreciated having the quiet time at home to do her work now that the youngest was also in school. Although she had a rather pretty face and an attractive full figure, Maggie never wore makeup and hid her body under baggy sweats, a clear indication that she had no time for men in her life. When I bothered to think about it, I considered it something of a shame that an intelligent, attractive woman would lead a life without a significant other. But I could understand how having once stuck your hand in the flame of a bad relationship you might be reluctant to do so a second time.

Maggie hopped up from the sofa and picked up the two bags.

"I'd better get on with this. The kids are at sports practice. Josh has soccer and Kim has field hockey. That should help them work off some of their excess energy. Josh gets to kick people and Kim hits them with sticks, so they usually come home mellow."

I laughed. "That makes me really look forward to having children."

Maggie gave me a sideways glance. "Are you thinking about it?"

"We have for quite a while now, but we kept putting it off because Jonathan wanted to have a novel published before there was a baby in the house to serve as a distraction."

"Well, if this Harrison Cole thing comes through, maybe the two of you can get right on it. After all, you'll have enough money to hire a nanny to do all the dirty work. I could have used one for a couple of years early on."

As I held the front door for Maggie and said goodbye, I wondered if Jonathan would be more amenable to starting a family if he got this job. That was something to think about.

JONATHAN DIDN'T ARRIVE home until the middle of the afternoon, and I could immediately tell by his red face and tight lips that things hadn't gone well. He collapsed in a kitchen chair and had the petulant expression on his face that told me he was just waiting for me to ask how things had gone so he could unleash a torrent of complaints. I decided to focus on the most important thing first.

"Have you had any lunch?" I asked.

He nodded. "We ordered from room service," he said, clearly annoyed that his tirade would have to wait a few seconds.

I sat down in a chair on the opposite side of the table and braced myself. "So how did things go?" I asked softly.

"The woman thinks she's a writer," Jonathan exploded. "I sent her what I had written last night, and by the time I got there this morning, she'd been through it all with a fine-tooth comb. She'd just about line edited the entire thing, and apparently thinks she's a developmental editor as well because she had unending questions about continuity, structure, and character development. It was a horror show."

"Maybe she's just a bit overly protective of her grandfather's reputation and doesn't trust the publisher to do a good job."

"It's more than that. She was an English major in college, and she's always been a frustrated writer. I don't think she can believe that her grandfather, whom she adored, would pick me to carry on his legacy instead of her. I'm convinced *she* wants to be the next Harrison Cole," he said, staring at me with panic in his eyes.

"Lynn Samson wouldn't let her get away with that."

"Why not?" Jonathan shouted. "Think about it from a marketing point of view. Who would attract more Cole readers, some guy no one has heard of or his beautiful young granddaughter. Hell, if I were in the marketing department for a big publisher, I'd pick her over me any day. Ultimately, Lynn will go along with whatever will get her a deal, and she'd be just as happy to represent Amanda as me."

"But I could tell that she didn't like Amanda."

"This is *business*. People don't decide based on likes and dislikes, they decide based on where the money is."

I sighed. I could see Jonathan's point. For once, he seemed to have thought a matter through clearly.

"How did you leave things with Amanda?"

"We went over the entire manuscript I'd sent her, and I listened to her pontificate on each little element she didn't like."

"Did you stay calm?"

"More or less. But I'm sure she could tell that I wasn't happy about it. Finally, I said that I would go over all her notes and make some changes that we could discuss on Tuesday."

"Back at her hotel room?"

He nodded. "The thing is, I know that what I've written would thrill the old man."

"How can you know that?"

Jonathan paused as if he'd said too much. "I can tell from reading his books."

"But you've only read two of them."

"I read them carefully. You can learn a lot about an author if you do that."

"Okay. Why don't you take the rest of the day off? You can start on the revisions tomorrow. So, lie down now and see if you can get a little nap before supper?"

Jonathan and I stood up, and he gave me a brief, hopeless hug before going up the stairs to the bedroom. I sat down again at the table and contemplated what to do next.

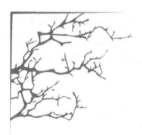

Chapter Five

I waited twenty minutes to give Jonathan enough time to fall asleep, then I quietly went up the stairs to the second floor. The door to our bedroom was closed, and I stood there for a minute to see if there were any sounds. Not hearing anything, I slowly made my way down the hall to Jonathan's study. Although he had never officially made a firm rule about it, I knew that he preferred I not go in there by myself, but this was a time when finding out what was happening outweighed the risk of getting him angry.

I went into the study and carefully opened the door to the closet, making sure not to allow it to squeak. Using the flashlight on my cell phone, I studied the box I had noticed earlier. Only one flap was up, but I could see that I had been correct and the books on top were by Harrison Cole. The other flap was sealed down with tape. Not deterred, I went over to Jonathan's desk and picked up the knife that Jonathan used to open his mail. He'd told me at one time that it was standard issue for the Navy SEALs. I'd considered it a bit absurd that a man who had never come closer to the military than playing combat video games as a teenager would use a deadly weapon as a letter opener, but I'd written it off as another manifestation of boys and their toys.

I carried the knife into the closet and quickly opened the box. There were fifteen books in the box, and a quick examination of the titles revealed that they were all Danforth novels. I picked out five and leafed through them quickly. Each contained marginal notes made by Jonathan commenting on the use of language and the style of writing. Since the books were covered with dust, they had clearly been in the closet for a while. I wondered when Jonathan had become so fascinated with the work of Harrison Cole and why. Perhaps it went back to their chance meeting at a conference, but Jonathan had passed that off as a casual conversation that led to no further contact. This box of books suggested that Jonathan's interest in the thriller author was of longer duration than two weeks. Even more disturbing to me was that it seemed to indicate that if Jonathan had not exactly lied to me, he had at least not told me the complete truth about his interest in Cole.

I knew that if I brought this up to Jonathan and told him I had gone into his study closet, he would be angry, but I also felt that if I didn't find out more about what was going on, there would be no way I could help him get the job writing the Danforth novels. If Jonathan insisted on keeping me in the dark, as he often liked to do, I'd be unable to assist him.

I put the box of books back in the closet, not bothering to seal it up again, then I went down to the kitchen and began to prepare dinner. I often found that cooking helped me think, and I knew that I had a lot of thinking to do. As I prepared the meal, I carefully reviewed the situation in my mind, looking for possible strategies that might help Jonathan work his way around the obstacle that Amanda posed.

When Jonathan came downstairs, he didn't come into the kitchen to greet me but took a seat in the living room instead. When I peaked in there a few minutes later, he was sitting in his easy chair staring at the rug as if the pattern might provide him with a solution to his problem. His silence was a sign to me of how seriously he was taking this dilemma because usually he would be buzzing around the kitchen as I tried to work, chattering about the day's events or putting forth one of his many opinions.

He ate his meal in a similar state of silence. Mechanically putting the food in his mouth and making no attempt at conversation. I didn't try to bring him out of his funk. This wasn't a time for trying to jolly him out of a bad mood. It was a time for getting the facts and coming up with a plan of action.

After eating, Jonathan went back to the living room. He didn't bother to turn on the television as he usually would, but instead returned to his chair and stared into space. When I was done cleaning up in the kitchen, I joined him and took my usual spot on the sofa. I waited to see if he was going to ask me for my advice, but he didn't. After ten minutes of sitting in silence, he started to stand.

"I'm going upstairs to my study," he announced.

"Sit down, please," I said.

Jonathan flopped back into the chair with a surprised expression on his face.

"Let's say you are correct, and that Amanda wants to become a writer and be the one to continue the Duke Danforth series. Do you seriously think that Lynn or the publisher is going to be happy with a completely untested young writer being given that kind of responsibility on her own?"

"Like I said, it would be good publicity to keep it in the family," he replied morosely.

"Perhaps. But allowing an untested writer to take on the job, especially when working with a short timeline, seems to be something that they would be reluctant to do. Whereas you say that you could do better."

"I can," he said in a hurt tone.

"You're a literary writer, Jonathan. Why are you so convinced that you can do the job?"

"I told you. It isn't that hard to imitate Cole's style."

"And how do you know that?"

"I'm a writer. I can easily figure that out by reading his books."

I sighed. "I found a box of Cole's Danforth novels in the back of the closet in your study. You've obviously been studying his novels for some time. Can you tell me why?"

"You went into my study without my permission," Jonathan said loudly, getting red in the face. "I've told you that's my *sanctum sanctorum*. The one place in the house where I need to have complete privacy."

"I was getting out a bag of clothes for giveaway and happened to see the box of books in the closet," I said, trying not to shrink back in the face of his anger. I continued in a trembling voice that I forced to remain steady. "Now I think you should tell me what's going on. If you don't, I won't be able to help you."

I could see him getting ready to respond angrily, probably to say that he didn't need my help. But then his face collapsed as he realized that he needed help from someone, and I was the only person available.

"I haven't been completely honest with you," he finally admitted, giving me one of his charming, sheepish smiles that always managed to get around me.

"In what way."

"When I met Harrison Cole at that conference, he was at a low point, and he really opened up to me. He told me that he was having great difficulty writing the next Duke Danforth novel. He admitted to being tired of writing them, and how he was finding it hard to become motivated since his wife had died. He was well past the deadline for submission, and Lynn Samson was telling him that if he didn't get something to her soon, it could seriously damage his career. He was depressed and in a panic."

"What did you say?" I asked.

"I expressed sympathy for his predicament, and suddenly, out of the blue, he suggested that I might co-write the novel with him. He even promised to give me equal credit on the cover. I told him openly that I had never written anything like that, but he insisted on sketching out the plot for me as far as he had developed it. He had the first five chapters done and notes for the rest. He assured me that if I read his previous books to get a sense of his style, it would be easy to complete the novel in a few months."

"And you agreed?"

He held out his hands in a pleading gesture. "What could I do? He was in a real fix, and I felt sorry for him. I'll admit that I also thought that this might be a way to put my name forward as a writer."

"So, you did what he asked?"

Jonathan nodded. "I read all the Duke Danforth's. Those are the books you found in the closet. As I said, it wasn't hard to get a sense of the old man's style. He gave me the first five chapters and his notes, and within three months, I'd completed the book for him. His publisher was ecstatic when he submitted it. The book came out a month ago and has sold well. No one apparently suspects that it wasn't written by Cole himself. So that's why I know I could easily take over writing his novels."

"But your name never got on the cover or else Lynn would have mentioned it."

Jonathan shrugged. "What can I say? I was naive. I should have had Cole put something in writing, but he seemed like such an honest guy. When the time came, he said that he just couldn't have the book attributed to me in any way. He was feeling better and thought that he could easily write more Danforth books by himself. He didn't want to break his string by having a co-writer on one of them. I couldn't do much because I had no proof of my involvement. He had insisted that all our communications either be in person or via snail mail, so there was no email record of our correspondence. There was no way I could prove that he hadn't written the book himself."

"Did he pay you?" Sarah asked.

"Oh, yes, I got quite a generous check when the book came out. And he did say one more thing. He said that he was so delighted with my work that he promised to put in his will that I should be given the first shot at carrying on the Danforth series."

Jonathan frowned and stared across the room.

"I was so angry with him at the time for leaving my name off the cover that I told him not to bother, and I stormed out. So, I really didn't think that he'd keep his promise. But I guess the old man had more integrity than I realized."

"When did all this take place?"

"I met him at the conference a little over a year ago. The book came out a month ago, and my last conversation with him was on the day I saw the book in the store without my name on it. That was three weeks ago."

I paused, wanting to make sure that my next words didn't make Jonathan angry or defensive.

"And why didn't you tell me about any of this?" I asked gently.

He ran his hands through his wavy hair and hung his head. "I know that I should have. But . . . I was ashamed. I've always been going on about how popular fiction is trash, and then here I am writing the stuff. I thought you'd lose all respect for me."

I walked across the room and knelt in front of him. I took his hands in mine.

"Of course I haven't lost respect for you. I think it's amazing that you were able to duplicate the work of such a popular author. That's something to be proud of. And who hasn't sometimes said one thing and done another. Most of us talk the talk more than we walk the walk."

Jonathan grinned. "I suppose you're right, darling."

"The important thing now is to turn this into a permanent gig, if that's what you want."

"It is. Oh, I know it won't get me into the highest literary circles, but at least I'll be known as a writer and not a dabbler. Plus, the money won't hurt either."

"What did you do with the money that Cole gave you?"

"I put it into an account in my name until I could figure out how to tell you about it."

"Well, Monday after school we'll close out that account and put it into our joint savings. No sense making our taxes more complicated than they must be."

He hesitated. "Sounds fine."

"I hope you get the job so you won't have to explain to those you've already told about it why the position didn't work out," I said with a note of admonishment. "Maggie mentioned to me today that you'd told her. Have you mentioned it to anybody else?"

"Some people at work. I know I was stupid, but I just couldn't contain my enthusiasm. You're right. It's going to be embarrassing if I have to go back to them and eat crow."

"Don't worry. We'll work something out."

Jonathan reached out and ruffled my hair. "You're taking this a lot better than I thought you would. I

45

know I should have told you all about it when the whole thing got started. I'm sorry."

I smiled and returned to the sofa. "The important thing right now is to come up with a way of dealing with Amanda."

"I don't think she's ever going to agree to let me write her grandfather's books. She really wants to do them herself. I wonder why her grandfather didn't choose her in the first place."

"He probably didn't like her as much as she thinks," I said. "People as self-centered as Amanda always believe that people adore them because they're oblivious to other people's true feelings."

"Maybe I could admit to Lynn that I wrote the last Danforth book. That would convince her that I'm capable of doing it. She might be able to pressure Amanda."

"But that would completely alienate Amanda, and I think you need both of them to get the job."

"So, what am I going to do?"

I stared into space for a moment, thinking.

"You know, Amanda may have an excessively high opinion of herself, but I think that on some level even she would be reluctant to take on this project by herself. She's in her midtwenties, with no professional writing experience, and a fast-approaching deadline. I think she knows that if you left her on her own, she'd sink under the pressure."

"Okay. Then what should I do?"

"I think you should offer to let her be your co-writer."

Jonathan frowned. "Oh, I don't know."

"It might even be better that way. As you said earlier, having the granddaughter's name on the cover would help sell books. Your name would be right under hers. That should be enough to secure your reputation as being a writer to watch. And everyone in the business is going to guess that you're the one doing the real writing."

Jonathan sat quietly for a moment. "That just might work."

"And you might only have to share the credit temporarily. Amanda's young and flighty. She'll soon be on to the next fun thing, so in another book or two, you might have all the credit to yourself."

"You're a genius, Sarah," Jonathan said, giving me one of his best smiles.

I smiled back. "I'm glad you've finally noticed."

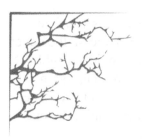

Chapter Six

J onathan spent most of his time on Sunday working on Amanda's corrections. I had suggested that taking her points seriously might help him to get on her good side and make her more amenable to sharing credit for the Duke Danforth novels. Although Jonathan was somewhat reluctant to consider Amanda's comments, I finally prevailed upon him to put his pride aside and do what would be most beneficial in the long run. He worked hard and by evening, he had incorporated most of her criticisms into the new draft of his partial manuscript. I hoped that would be enough to satisfy the privileged Miss Amanda.

The next day being Monday, we both had to go to work. After Jonathan got home in the late afternoon, we went to the bank and closed out the account he had opened in only his name. We deposited the money in our joint account. When I saw the deposit slip, my eyes opened wide.

"Harrison Cole paid you fifty thousand dollars for writing his last book," I said as we drove out of the bank parking lot. "That's a really good payday."

"Probably only a small fraction of the advance he got for it. The old boy was rolling in money."

"So, would you get even more for the next book?"

"Hard to know. I'd have to share with Amanda, but I'd guess I'd end up with at least as much if not more."

I was impressed and more determined than ever to solve the problem that Amanda presented. "Would you mind if I looked over the manuscript you're showing to Amanda tomorrow?"

"Why?" As usual, Jonathan was hesitant to show me his work.

"It might not hurt to have another woman read it over first. It could help you prepare for any new objections Amanda might have."

"Okay. That might be a good idea," he admitted after thinking about it.

That night, I pored over the seventy-five pages he gave me to read. I found the story very entertaining, although there were several changes I would have made. My only major suggestion was to strengthen the main female character so she'd be a better partner for the male lead. Jonathan scrunched up his nose a bit at the suggestion, but eventually he admitted that a strong female lead might help interest woman readers, which made good commercial sense.

I must admit that I was far less focused than usual on my teaching the next day as my mind kept wandering to what the outcome of Jonathan's meeting with Amanda might be. He was going to see her in the afternoon to propose their co-authorship and get her opinion of the revised manuscript. Although I had tried to project confidence to Jonathan that she would be happy with the plan, in my own mind I was far less certain that such a self-centered young woman would be able to compromise, even if it was in her self-interest.

I was in the middle of preparing dinner when Jonathan danced into the kitchen. He spun around twice and handed me a marvelous bouquet of roses.

"This is for my beautiful wife who is also a genius. You were so right. Amanda bought the plan hook, line, and sinker. She says that she'd be delighted to work with me and apologized for being so difficult last time. She said that she just resented being left out as a contributor to her grandfather's legacy, and she thinks we'll make splendid partners."

"What did she think of your rewrites?" I asked.

"Absolutely loved them, but you were right, she did want to see a stronger heroine. And thanks to you, I was ready with some suggestions. The whole thing couldn't have gone better. But I'll have to work hard tonight and in my spare time tomorrow because she wants to see five thousand more words by Thursday."

"Is she going to do any of the actual writing herself?"

He shook his head. "We decided that her contribution will be in suggesting changes and coming up with ideas about plot development. She's willing to leave the actual writing to me."

"Are you happy with that?" I asked.

He nodded. "Relieved, to be honest. It puts more of the burden on me, but I think it will probably be the smoothest way to do things. It's hard to know how we could divide up the writing if we each did our own part, and the continuity of style would probably suffer."

"So, you think you can work with her?"

"Sure. She seems to have warmed to the idea of a collaboration, and she isn't stupid. Actually, Amanda can be quite charming when she isn't getting upset about someone cutting her out of her grandfather's legacy."

I knew Jonathan well enough to realize that his opinion of Amanda had changed dramatically for the better. That raised problems of its own.

JONATHAN RETURNED TO working steadily on the manuscript. He would go up to his study right after supper and often come to bed so late that I wouldn't hear him. On the rare occasions when I dared to ask him how the work was going, he said that it was proceeding well, and that he and Amanda had developed an amicable working relationship. He was spending at least three hours a day with her twice a week, and I was beginning to wonder once again whether it was a good idea to have Jonathan exposed to a young, attractive woman who would probably have no compunction about seducing him. Granted, he was a few years older than she, but that might just make him more attractive to her.

Two weeks later, on a Saturday, I had gotten myself so worked up that I spent most of the afternoon preparing a lavish meal for dinner, even going so far as to bake an apple pie, Jonathan's favorite.

When I got a call from Jonathan at five o'clock saying that he and Amanda were in the midst of a creative flow and didn't want to end the session until they'd reached the conclusion of the next section, I was irate.

"You should have called me sooner. Then I wouldn't have prepared so much for dinner," I snapped.

"Sorry," he said, not really sounding sorry at all. "We didn't know that the ideas would be coming like this. If we stop now, they might be gone by tomorrow. Writing doesn't always keep to a timetable."

"Well, I do," I said, ending the call.

I immediately regretted being so childishly rude. It had nothing to do with delaying dinner, of course, but was simply the culmination of weeks of suspicion that more than writing was going on in that hotel room. I turned off the food and went out into the living room to sulk. I knew that Jonathan was probably behaving himself, but the image in my mind of perfect little Amanda was driving me up the wall. Then the doorbell rang.

Maggie was on the front porch. "Sorry to bother you, and this may seem foolish, but I can't remember whether this is the week our side of the street recycles." She laughed. "I think my memory is completely shot."

"It's next week," I said, a bit more abruptly than I intended.

Maggie took a close look at me. "Are you okay? You seem a bit . . . agitated."

I was going to say that everything was fine, but then I suddenly decided that discussing the matter with someone a few years older who had once dealt with a philandering husband might not be a bad idea.

"Do you have a minute?" I asked.

She nodded. "I'm sure my kids won't burn down the house in the next fifteen minutes."

We went into the living room and sat next to each other on the sofa. We were both silent for a moment. I wasn't accustomed to sharing my problems with others and not certain how to begin.

"Well, you already know about Jonathan writing the next Harrison Cole novel," I began.

She smiled. "And it sounds like a great opportunity for him."

"Yes, well it seems that Cole's granddaughter is insisting that she and Jonathan write it together, and they've been working steadily in her hotel room for the last two weeks."

"I see."

Now that I'd come to the crux of the problem, I found it hard to go on.

"What does this granddaughter look like?" Maggie asked, as though trying to ease me into the conversation.

"She's a beautiful young woman in her midtwenties who thinks she's a little princess. Frankly, I think she's on the prowl for any good-looking guy she can find, whether he's married or not."

"And you're afraid she's set her cap for Jonathan?"

"He's attractive, a bit older, and talented. I think that's catnip to her."

Maggie paused. "Do you have evidence that anything is going on between them?"

"No, none at all," I said quickly. "And that's what makes the whole thing so hard. I don't want Jonathan to think I don't trust him, and if I start interrogating him, it will hurt his feelings and maybe send him into her arms. But I feel so helpless just sitting here while they're doing God knows what."

"Don't you trust Jonathan?"

"I do, but I guess this is a case where I'd like it to be able to trust and then verify. I'd like some way of being sure that my confidence isn't being misplaced. I just got a call saying he won't be home for dinner because they're working into the night, and it's really messing with my head."

She nodded.

"Do you think I'm being silly, and I should do nothing?" I smiled. "If only Jonathan weren't such a good-looking guy."

"That doesn't matter. My husband was certainly nothing special to look at, but he gave out high-pitched signals, like a dog whistle, that any woman looking for action could hear. It must have been enticing because they gathered around like moths to a flame. It's more than looks; it's availability."

"I don't think Jonathan gives out those vibes," I said doubtfully.

Maggie grinned. "I've never noticed, but then I don't pay attention to that kind of thing anymore."

"So, are you saying that I should play the dutiful wife?"

"No, too many marriages have ended up on the rocks because the wife was too polite for her own good."

Maggie suddenly took in a deep breath and smiled.

"You've been baking, haven't you?" she asked.

I nodded impatiently. "That's what makes this even worse. I made a special dinner for us, and now he won't be home to eat any of it. I even made an apple pie for him. It's his favorite." I knew I sounded pathetic, but that was how I felt.

"I have an idea how you can find out if anything is going on without making any hurtful accusations."

"How?"

"Bring a couple of pieces of that pie to them tonight. You can always give the excuse that you thought that since they were working so hard, they might appreciate a special dessert. That way you can check on what they're up to while sounding like you're doing the whole thing out of the goodness of your heart."

I considered her idea, wondering whether I had the acting skills to carry it off. It was going to be a challenge to make my concern for their well-being sound sincere. But I couldn't think of a better plan, and I was desperate.

"I'll give it a try," I said.

"Good," Maggie said, standing up. "I'd better get home to check on my little rascals. Good luck and I hope it all works out for you."

"Thanks for all your help," I said, giving her a brief hug.

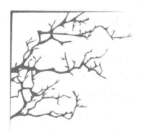

Chapter Seven

I knew that Amanda was staying in an old, rather grand hotel in the center of Great Barrington. I'd been to eat in the restaurant once, so I knew how to get there. I found a parking spot on the street right around the corner. It was a blustery, cool October night. The wind blowing through the trees giving a hint of Halloween soon to come. There's something about fall nights in the Berkshires that conjure up in my mind headless horsemen and witches on brooms. It's almost like I can feel the way the first settlers did upon arriving in a strange wild land and being confronted with nothing but forests and the darkness of the unknown.

As I entered the lobby of the hotel, I realized that I had no idea what room Amanda was staying in, so I'd have to ask at the desk. A young woman wearing an unbecoming maroon blazer that must have been part of the official uniform, looked up at me as I approached the reservations desk and smiled politely.

"I'm here to see Amanda Beaumont. Can you tell me her room number please?"

She studied me standing there in my jeans and flannel shirt, carrying a plate in one hand, and quickly arrived at a conclusion.

"I'm sorry. It's not our policy to give out guest's room numbers. But I can call her room and see if she'd like to see you."

I frowned. By the time I got to their room, they could have dressed and arranged the room to make everything appear innocent. I wouldn't be catching them unaware. But I didn't seem to have a choice.

"Would you please do that?" I asked.

She nodded, checked on her computer, and punched buttons on her phone.

"Hello, Ms. Beaumont, there's a . . ." she paused to glance at me questioningly.

"Sarah McAdams."

"There's a Sarah McAdams here to see you. Shall I send her up."

Apparently, she got permission because she turned to me and said, "That will be room 315."

I nodded and walked to the elevator behind me, imagining all the while the flurry of activity in 315 as the two of them scrambled around finding items of clothing and straightening the bed. I got off the elevator and almost ran down the hall to 315, nearly dropping my pie.

I knocked on the door. After a few seconds, it opened, and Jonathan stood in the doorway.

"Why are you here?" he asked in a less than friendly tone.

I stepped forward into the room, almost brushing him aside. I immediately turned my attention toward the bed. It appeared to be neatly made with no signs

57

that it had been urgently restored to some semblance of order after hours of passionate lovemaking.

I gave him what I hoped was a convincing smile. "I baked an apple pie, and I thought the two of you might enjoy a homemade dessert after a day of hard work."

"Thank you," Jonathan said with a neutral expression.

Amanda had been standing all this time on the far side of the room. She pointed regally to a small empty space on the top of the desk that occupied one wall of the room. The rest of it was covered with manuscript pages. "You may place it there," she said.

I put the plate in the spot indicated and pulled two forks out of my coat pocket.

"How's the writing going?" I asked

"Pretty well," Jonathan said.

I looked at Amanda to see if she would respond, but she was busy staring at me with a knowing, even mocking, smile on her face, as if she knew exactly why I had appeared in their hotel room.

"Well, that's good," I said weakly. "I'll leave you to it then. Enjoy the pie."

"Thanks again," Jonathan called out as I left the room.

I walked down the richly carpeted hall, blushing and glad that no one could see. My cheeks burned every time I visualized the haughty expression on Amanda's face. Although I don't think of myself as a violent person, I could easily imagine myself punching my fist into her perfect little nose.

As I drove back home, I did find a bit of a silver lining on the rather bleak cloud of humiliation. There had been no sign that they were doing anything other than working on the next Harrison Cole book. Of course, it was always possible that they frolicked first and then wrote. Who knows with writers? Sex may have served as a sort of foreplay to the real fun. But to anyone who was objective, which I admitted didn't include myself, there was no sign of hanky-panky. So, I told myself, I should calm down and cool my mental jets of jealousy. Although I found Amanda reprehensible, that was no reason to doubt Jonathan or to foul up his opportunity for literary success.

I went to bed early, and although I tossed and turned for a while, I was fortunately sound asleep when Jonathan returned.

THE NEXT MORNING, I was up early. Jonathan was sleeping peacefully next to me as I made my way to the bathroom. I stared at my reflection in the mirror. The woman I saw didn't look half bad. Oh, there were fine lines next to the eyes that I liked to think of as laugh lines, and a few more wrinkles on the forehead than a few years ago. I may have put on a pound or two since our marriage and developed the occasional gray hair, but basically, I thought I looked pretty good for thirty-two. Of course, there was the rub. I was thirty-two, not twenty-five, and I'd never been a great beauty like Amanda in the first place. But why should this even be a competition? After all, I was Jonathan's wife. There was no reason why I had to win a beauty contest against his colleague. Or did I?

I had finished my breakfast and begun puttering around in the kitchen when Jonathan put in an appearance.

"How did things go after I left last night?" I asked.

"We worked until eleven. It was a slog, but I think we've got a good draft of the first two-thirds of the novel. We'll have to do some fine tuning after we finish the whole thing, of course, but right now it's encouraging."

"Does Amanda feel the same way?"

He nodded. "She's happy with what I've been writing, and I must admit that her comments have been invaluable. She certainly has a flair for the dramatic in writing."

And in real life as well, I thought to myself.

Jonathan poured himself a cup of coffee and settled down at the table.

"Thanks for the apple pie last night," he said. "Amanda thought that maybe you came by to check up on us to see that we were really working. I told her not to be silly, that you weren't that sort of suspicious wife."

I worked on presenting a surprised smile. "I wonder why she would think that. I just thought you would both enjoy a homemade dessert."

"That's what I told her." He paused. "I know that Amanda is young and attractive but for me this is a working relationship. I have to get along with her if I'm going to write the Harrison Cole novels, and we both want that, don't we?"

"Of course."

He nodded and went to the closet to get a bowl and some cereal. The matter clearly settled in his mind.

"When do you two get back together again?" I asked causally.

"Tuesday. That means I have today and when I'm not teaching tomorrow to work on the final third of the novel. We sketched out some of the remaining scenes, but the hard work remains to be done."

"Will you be back at her hotel room, then?" I figured that I knew the room number now, and if necessary, I could do an unannounced visit. I'd have two days to come up with an adequate excuse.

"No. She's moving into her grandfather's cottage tomorrow."

"Doesn't she already have a place to live?"

"She has an apartment down in Manhattan, but I think she's planning to stay up here at least until Thanksgiving. But she'll probably keep the place to use as a summer home."

"Very nice."

I vacuumed the living room rug while Jonathan ate his breakfast. When he stepped into the doorway and announced that he was going upstairs to write, I knew that was the signal that I had to stop making noise and find something less noisy to do. I did a bit of random dusting around the downstairs and considered whether I should go in the dining room and devote some time to answering emails and working on lesson plans. However, I felt too restless to sit down and write, so I put on my walking shoes and headed out the front door for a stroll around the neighborhood. Maggie was in her front yard raking leaves, so I called out hello and walked across the lawn to speak with her.

"I went to the hotel last night," I said.

She nodded and held up a hand. "You don't have to tell me anything. This is your personal business."

"I just want you to know that it appears nothing inappropriate is going on, although I can't be positive."

"Why not?"

I explained about them having a few minutes warning of my arrival.

"Still, it sounds as though it's all pretty innocent," she said with a soothing smile.

"I suppose."

"Why do you still have doubts?"

I shrugged. "It's subtle, but I think Jonathan is starting to be impressed by her literary ability. He's gone from being certain that she would be no help at all to thinking that her help is essential."

"Is that really something to worry about? I mean, isn't it good that they're able to work together," Maggie said.

I frowned and struggled to put my thoughts into words. "With most men, looks would be the most important aspect of what a woman has to offer, but for someone like Jonathan it's their mind. Oh, I'm not saying that beauty doesn't matter to him, but Amanda is starting to sound like the entire package. That's what's got me worried. Jonathan might find it hard to justify cheating on me just for sex, but if it would also improve his writing, that would make it a lot easier for him to justify an affair to himself."

Maggie nodded and looked serious. "I see your point."

"Oh, well," I said with forced brightness. "Pretty soon the book will be done. That will end their working together, at least for a while. And there was probably nothing there to begin with."

I gave Maggie a wave and headed out for my walk hoping that my optimistic spin on the matter would prove accurate.

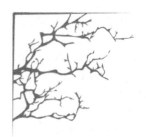

Chapter Eight

The next week went by uneventfully. Jonathan was working hard every night after dinner in his study. He met with Amanda at the Cole cottage on Tuesday and Thursday. I refrained from asking many questions so as not to appear to be the jealous wife. He seemed happy and his mood was gentle, which was usually an indication that the writing was going well. Friday night before he went up to his study, he announced that he would also be spending Saturday afternoon with Amanda.

I nodded with apparent indifference. "Are you making progress?"

"We're about three-quarters done with the first draft. Once the final quarter is complete, all that remains is to polish it and send the manuscript off to Lynn for her comments and approval." Jonathan paused for a moment. "Of course, all of that depends on whether Amanda is satisfied with the finished product."

"I thought you two were of one mind about how this was going."

"Well, I *think* we are, but with Amanda it's sometimes hard to tell. She's a bit moody, you know.

She'll sound really excited about the story one day and be kind of down on it the next. When I ask her what's wrong with it, she'll smile enigmatically like I should already know. But I'm not a mind reader. If she's unhappy about something, she has to tell me."

I felt a clenching in my gut that told me her unhappiness was less tied to the story than to the failure of her seduction of Jonathan to get any traction. But I knew that if I told him that, he would accuse me of being silly or worse of being a suspicious shrew. This was something he would have to learn for himself. All I could do is hope he made the right decision.

I spent Saturday morning shopping for food to keep busy outside of the house so I wouldn't be tempted to discuss Jonathan's situation with him. I had arranged to have lunch with some teacher friends at a local restaurant because I thought it would be a good distraction from all of my jealous worrying. I stood in Jonathan's study door as I got ready to leave and wished him a productive afternoon. He got up and walked around his desk to give me a kiss on the lips, which I took to be a good sign.

"Pretty soon this will all be over," he said with a smile.

"Of course it will."

At least, I certainly hoped it would.

I HAD A GOOD TIME WITH my friends at lunch and was not surprised when I returned home at four to find that Jonathan wasn't there. I fully expected that he would put in another late night working with Amanda. One of the advantages of having a large lunch was that I didn't have to worry about preparing dinner. A yogurt would suffice. So, I was startled when I heard a key in the front door around seven. Coming out of the kitchen, I saw Jonathan walking unsteadily down the hallway. He staggered slightly, and at first, I thought he was drunk.

"You're home early," I said.

He didn't respond. Instead, he walked into the living room and collapsed into his easy chair without even removing his coat.

"What's the matter?" I asked, alarmed.

"It's all over. I'm not going to get the job as the next Harrison Cole."

"Why not?"

He looked up at me, and I could see the tears in his eyes. But I couldn't tell if they were tears of disappointment or something else.

"What's happened?"

He took a deep, shuttering breath. "Amanda. She said she wanted to sleep with me. I told her I wasn't interested, and she went ballistic. She began yelling at the top of her lungs about how I should be the one begging her to have sex. And then she told me to get out, that she'd finish the book herself without my help. I told her that I was the one who had written it, and she said that she'd send it to Lynn and tell her it was her own work. She said that there was no way I could prove differently. I pointed out that there was a quarter of the book left to write, and she didn't have the ability to finish one paragraph of it."

"What did she say to that?" I asked.

"She said that there were lots of hack writers around. Lynn could easily find someone who would be willing to finish it with her. Then she started throwing things at me. I was furious and afraid that I'd do something I'd regret, so I left."

"So, you came home?"

He shook his head. "I left, but I drove around for a while trying to clear my head. I thought about going back and attempting to work things out. But she was crazy, so I decided to leave it until tomorrow. I figured maybe this was just one of her passing moods."

"Maybe seeing her tomorrow is the best idea."

"I'm not sure. What if she calls Lynn tonight? I might be out of a job already. But I'm afraid that if I go back to talk to her, she'll go nuts all over again."

"How about if I went to see her?" I asked.

It was low on my list of things to do, but I knew how much this writing gig meant to Jonathan, and Amanda might not get as angry talking to another woman. Plus, she probably had too much contempt for me to even bother throwing me out of her house.

"Would you do that?" Jonathan asked hopefully. "I really want this deal to work out."

I gave him an encouraging smile. "Of course I will."

"I think I'll go upstairs and lie down for a while. This whole thing has got me kind of upset."

"Good idea," I said, getting my coat and heading for the door. "How about giving me some directions to the cottage from the center of Great Barrington?" Jonathan rattled off a couple of street names and landmarks. I jotted them down.

Cole's cottage turned out to be quite a way out of the center of Great Barrington on a rural road. The driveway to the house meandered up a hill before depositing me in front of a large, two-story, wood-shingled building. It was certainly larger than anything I would describe as a cottage and a foreboding presence in the darkness against the backdrop of the hill behind it.

I had become concerned on the ride out that Amanda might not be home and my half-hour journey would be to no purpose. But there was a light shining through the double windows to the left side of the front door, so it appeared I was in luck. I sat there for a moment wondering how to approach the matter. During the drive, I had begun to have doubts as to the wisdom of my confronting Amanda this evening while she was still so angry with Jonathan. Maybe giving her some time to cool down would be a better idea. But Jonathan was right. If she was that angry, she might well call Lynn and put in motion some plan to have him removed from the writing team. I had to cut that off at the pass if possible. I could only hope that she wouldn't start throwing things at me.

I walked across to the sweeping front veranda, up the stairs to the double door. I was about to knock when I saw that the doors were ajar. I smiled slightly to myself. Apparently, Jonathan truly had beat a hasty retreat. The notion of that small young woman throwing things at him tickled my fancy. I pushed the door open but didn't hear any sounds.

"Hello, Amanda," I called out. "It's Sarah McAdams. Is it okay if I come in to talk with you?"

There was no reply. That didn't necessarily mean she was ignoring me. It was a large house. She could be upstairs in the back and not hear me, and I couldn't tell if there were lights on up there from the driveway.

"Amanda," I called out loud in that artificial voice we use when not certain that anyone is there to listen.

There was still no response. Perhaps she had gone out and left the light burning. She might do that for security purposes or simply out of neglectfulness. Amanda didn't strike me as someone who worried much about wasting watts. I debated whether I should turn around and go back home with my mission unaccomplished. I was tempted. The day had caught up with me and I was tired, not sure I would be able to deal with a feisty Amanda. But then the importance of this matter reasserted itself, and I decided to make more of an effort. I opened the door wider and stepped into the front hallway. Off to the left side was a sweeping wooden staircase that led up to the second floor, and at the foot of it was the lighted doorway into a room. I slowly walked toward the light.

"Amanda," I said yet again. And again, I received no answer.

I forged ahead into the room. The back of a sofa was directly in front of me and to the right was a large fieldstone fireplace with two wingback chairs on either side of the firebox. I could see a desk with a computer on it along the far wall, and there was a table with papers scattered over the surface. This was clearly the room where Amanda and Jonathan had been working.

I walked around the sofa, then stopped. Amanda was lying in the middle of the wood floor, face down.

Her skimpy sundress was hiked up revealing the backs of her flawless thighs. It wasn't a bad look for her, but as my gaze slowly went higher, her badly battered head spoiled the picture. A large pool of blood had spread out across the room, reaching as far as the rug between the chairs.

I staggered backward, gasping for air. I turned and ran out into the hallway and stood there for a time hyperventilating. When I finally got my breath under control, I stood as quietly as possible for a moment trying to decide what to do. My initial instinct was to run as far away from the scene as possible. For the first time, I understood why innocent people who come across a crime scene often do stupid things that make them appear guilty. The desire to escape the horror can often get in the way of common sense.

But I continued standing there, repeating to myself, "Don't do anything until you've had time to think." After a few moments, my brain began to reengage. It might seem that I could just drive away, and no one would be the wiser. But I knew from watching television that, even in rural areas, there was always a nosey neighbor who wrote down license plate numbers for a hobby or an unfortunately located security camera that had captured a great shot of my face. I hadn't done anything wrong, so it was best to immediately phone the police and report what I'd found. Under the circumstances, it was always a possibility that I would be considered a suspect, but I preferred to be the suspect who had notified the police of the crime than the one who had run away and been captured.

I went outside, took out my phone, and called 911.

I WAS SITTING ACROSS the hall from the room where I had found Amanda. It turned out to be a living room with another large fireplace and several conversation areas. Harrison Cole had certainly spared no expense on his cottage. The Duke Danforth novels must indeed have paid well. The uniformed officer who had first responded to my call had told me to wait outside, while he checked inside. He came back looking rather shaken and in urgent tones called for backup. Finally, someone else in uniform who was addressed as "sergeant" told me I could wait in this room since it was getting quite cold outside. He came in a few minutes later and asked me to give him an account of the events leading up to my discovery of the body. I did so. He took down notes in a small pad and told me to wait where I was because a detective was on the way to question me.

As I waited, there was considerable bustling around out in the hall. From my limited vantage point, I saw several officers in uniform and others wearing plastic suits going in and out of what I thought of as the murder room. There was also a great deal of chatter, some of it related to business and some surprisingly idle given the gravity of the situation.

I sat there for about an hour until a man in his forties, not much taller than myself with curly brown hair and wearing a rumpled raincoat, walked into the

71

room and introduced himself as Lieutenant Cranston. I smiled to myself at the thought that he clearly had spent too much time watching *Columbo* reruns. He sat down in a leather chair across from me. I thought he would probably ask me to give my account of events once again. Cops on television always did that, attempting to catch a witness in a lie. But instead, he smiled.

"It's been a tough night, hasn't it?"

"Yes."

"You told the sergeant who spoke to you that you came here to talk to Ms. Beaumont about a book she's writing with your husband?"

I nodded. "They were working as a team to write the next Duke Danforth thriller. Amanda Beaumont, of course, is his granddaughter, and my husband is a writer."

"Great! I'm glad they're planning to continue that series. I love those books. They have great plots— very twisty." He gave a small apologetic smile. "Intriguing to someone in my line of work."

"I can understand that."

"You told the officer that your husband came home at what time?"

"Around seven o'clock."

"And he reported that he and Ms. Beaumont had experienced a disagreement of some sort."

"Yes. They'd had some creative differences."

"I see. I imagine that, as a professional writer, your husband was doing the lion's share of the work."

"They were both making their own contributions. I believe Amanda's were focused more on plotting and critiquing than on the actual writing."

"Okay. And that's where the disagreements arose."

I paused for a moment. I had been rather sketchy in what I had said to the uniformed officer on this point, but Jonathan was a terrible liar. If I didn't tell the truth here, he might well blurt it out what really happened and make me look like a suspect. Once again, it was best to be truthful.

"I think their disagreement was more personal. My husband told me that Amanda wanted him to sleep with her, and he refused. That led to an argument which became heated on her part."

"A woman scorned?"

"I suppose you could say that."

"And what did she say when he refused her?"

"She threatened to have him replaced as the writer of the Duke Danforth series."

"Could she do that?" Cranston asked.

I shrugged. "She didn't have the final say, but Amanda certainly could have made things difficult for him. I think she would be a rather vindictive woman if thwarted."

The lieutenant gazed off into space. "Although it's a bit difficult to tell under the circumstances, Ms. Beaumont appears to have been a very attractive young woman. So, it must have been comforting to you when your husband came home and told you that he had turned down her advances."

"I've never had reason to doubt my husband's faithfulness."

He nodded. "And what was your purpose in making the trip out here to see Ms. Beaumont?"

"I was hoping to prevent her from acting on her plan to have him removed from the writing project."

"How were you planning to manage that?"

"I thought that I could reason with her and get her to see that replacing my husband at such a late stage would make it difficult to get the book completed on time."

"So, you didn't come here because you were furious with her for trying to seduce your husband?" he asked, suddenly staring at my face as if he could read my inner thoughts.

"No. Are you trying to make me into a suspect?" I asked, feeling a tightness in my chest.

He smiled. "Just checking. But I don't really suspect you. Preliminary reports indicate that Ms. Beaumont died between four-thirty and six. So, if you only arrived around eight, you're in the clear. For the record, however, where were you between four-thirty and six?"

"I had lunch with friends at a restaurant from one until three-thirty. I arrived home at four and stayed there until I left to come here at around seven-thirty."

"So, you have no alibi for the time in question. You could have driven here, waited outside until your husband left at five, and then murdered Ms. Beaumont. You'd have had time to get home before your husband arrived at seven."

"I suppose that's true. But until my husband came home at seven and told me what had happened, I had no reason to kill Amanda. As far as I knew, she and my husband had a perfectly proper professional relationship."

He nodded. "Good point. Perhaps you should be the one writing the Duke Danforth novels. Where is your husband at this time?"

"As far as I know he's at home, and probably wondering what happened to me. Would it be okay if I called him?"

The lieutenant stood up and indicated that I should do so as well.

"Why don't we go visit your husband together?"

"It's past ten o'clock. Couldn't this wait until tomorrow?"

"Are you okay to drive yourself?"

I nodded.

"Then why don't you lead the way. My sergeant and I will follow. Would you mind if I held onto your phone until we reach your house?"

I handed him the phone, figuring he didn't want me notifying Jonathan of our arrival.

"Take it slow and stay calm," Cranston said, as he escorted me out the front door.

I hoped that I could follow that guidance.

Chapter Nine

I was jumpy for the entire drive home. The shock of finding Amanda's body was starting to set in and my hands began to shake on the steering wheel. Despite Cranston's lukewarm assurances, I still wasn't convinced that he didn't consider me his prime suspect. He was right that I didn't have an alibi for the time of the murder, and he might suspect that I had prior reasons to suspect that Amanda was interested in my husband for other than professional reasons. If he ever talked to the clerk at the hotel in Great Barrington, I could easily come off as being a woman driven by jealousy.

When I finally pulled into the driveway at home, I sat there and took several deep breaths to regain my equilibrium. I was still sitting there when I head a knock on the window.

"Are you all right?" Lieutenant Cranston asked. He looked genuinely concerned.

I nodded and climbed out of the car. We walked up to the front door in a line with me leading, followed closely by the lieutenant, and another man in plain clothes, who had been introduced to me as Sergeant Hoffman. I could have used my key and walked right in, but I wanted Jonathan to have some warning, so I rang the bell. It took a couple of minutes and a few more rings of the bell before the door opened revealing Jonathan in his pajamas and robe, looking like he'd been sound asleep. It was good to know that he had been anxiously waiting up to see how I had made out with his crazy girlfriend.

"Did you forget . . ." He began, then froze when he saw the men behind me.

I made the introductions, and after a bit of milling around in the small hallway, we all made our way into the living room.

"Why are the police here?" Jonathan asked me.

"I'm sorry to have to inform you that Amanda Beaumont was found murdered in her home this evening," Lieutenant Cranston said.

Jonathan looked at me with the accusation clear in his eyes. He couldn't have put more blame on me if he had shouted, "Why did you do it!"

"Your wife found the victim's body and notified the police. We'd like to know what time you left Ms. Beaumont's house."

Jonathan licked his lips nervously. "It was around five. I think the mantle clock in the study had chimed five just before I left."

"Would that be shortly after the disagreement over whether you would have sexual relations with her?"

Jonathan glared at me. If I hadn't told the truth, he probably would have made up some blatantly transparent lie that would have gotten him in even more hot water. For a storyteller, he was an incredibly bad liar.

He lowered his head. "Yes. She apparently saw our relationship developing in a different direction than I did."

"And did Ms. Beaumont become violent?"

"I wouldn't say that, but she was certainly agitated."

"Did she shout at you, throw things, threaten to have you removed from the Danforth writing project?" Cranston asked in his calm, reasonable voice.

"Yes," Jonathan muttered.

"That must have gotten you angry."

"Sure, it did. That's why I left."

"Did you see anyone else in the area when you were leaving her home this evening?"

He shook his head.

"Are you certain? Because from the timeline we're currently working with, you were the last person to see her alive."

"Aside from the murderer," I put in.

Cranston ignored me and stared at my husband.

"I didn't see anyone," Jonathan repeated. "But I was upset and didn't spend time looking around."

"Okay. You left Ms. Beaumont's place shortly after five o'clock, but you didn't reach your home until seven. What were you doing for the intervening two hours?"

"Driving."

"Where to?"

"Just around. A lot of times when I need to think, I just drive nowhere in particular."

"That's true," I threw in.

"You must have gone somewhere," the lieutenant insisted.

"I took the backroads home from Great Barrington, took a drive around Pittsfield, then came back here."

"And that's when you told your wife what had happened?"

Jonathan nodded.

"You know, Amanda Beaumont didn't live in the area. She'd only been staying up here temporarily while working on the book," I pointed out.

Cranston nodded. "Her driver's license shows an address in Manhattan."

"That's only a little over three hours away. Maybe she had an enemy down in the city who came up here to kill her."

The lieutenant smiled. "We're going to be looking into that. Don't worry. We'll leave no stone unturned."

"I hope not," I said.

Cranston took two cards out of the pocket of his raincoat and handed one to each of us. "Please give me a call if you plan to leave town or if anything else about tonight's events occurs to you."

"We can't leave town?" Jonathan asked, startled. "Does that mean we're suspects?"

"It just means that you are both material witnesses in a murder case, and we like to know where we can reach you if necessary."

Jonathan looked unconvinced. And I must admit, I felt the same way.

"We'll be in touch," Cranston promised as he and the sergeant left the room.

I waited until I heard the door close, then I went out into the hall to lock it. When I got back to the living room, Jonathan was staring at the floor with his head in his hands.

"Did you have to tell them that Amanda and I had a fight?" he whined.

"How was I supposed to explain why I went to see her? We weren't exactly best friends who got together regularly for a drink."

"You should have just left when you walked in and found the body. You didn't have to alert the police."

"Right. Like that wouldn't look suspicious if anyone had spotted me." I paused for a moment. "You know, I've just experienced finding the body of someone I knew who was brutally murdered. You might show a little concern for me instead of just worrying about yourself."

A stricken look came over his face. He came across and sat down next to me on the sofa.

"You're right. I'm acting like a jerk." He put his arm around me. "I'm sorry you had to go through that, and I appreciate that it wouldn't have happened if you weren't helping me."

We sat there for a moment, enjoying the closeness.

"You know I didn't kill her, don't you?" Jonathan asked.

"Of course, you couldn't kill anyone," I said with more certainty than I felt.

"And I know you didn't kill her either," he replied.

"So, there we are, then," I said, sure that he was about as certain of my innocence as I was of his.

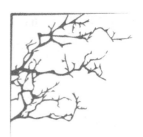

Chapter Ten

The next week passed uneventfully. For the first three days, Jonathan moped around the house when he wasn't teaching, saying he didn't see any point in working on the novel now that Amanda was gone. He thought that Lynn would probably cancel the project entirely or seek out someone else to continue with it. That usually led to Jonathan ranting about how he would refuse to send her the draft manuscript if he wasn't allowed to finish the book.

"That's my work," he'd shout. "And I'll be damned if I'm going to give it to Lynn to pass on to some hack who thinks he can do better."

I tuned out what he had to say. I wasn't certain what Lynn was going to do, but I saw no point in getting excessively agitated in advance. It turned out that I was right because on day four Lynn did call. She asked Jonathan how much progress had been made on the novel. When he told her that two-thirds of the book was already in the form of a good first draft, she suggested that he carry on with the writing by himself. Lynn expressed confidence that if she approved it, the publisher would have no objections to putting it out.

Jonathan's demeanor quickly brightened. He decided to go through the entire manuscript again and undo many of the changes that Amanda had suggested which he thought weakened the story, and then he would push on to the end. I breathed a sigh of relief. A Jonathan with hope for the future was a big improvement over the opposite.

One of the advantages of having the police visit your home late at night in an unmarked car is that the neighbors have no idea that anything untoward has happened. No gossip circulated around the neighborhood that Jonathan or I were involved in any kind of criminal activity, and the police had kept most details of Amanda Beaumont's death out of the newspaper. I think both of us were lulled into thinking that either the murder would never be solved and would gradually disappear into a cold case file in the basement of the police station, or that it would turn out that her killer was someone from down in the wicked big city.

So, I felt no trepidation at all in deciding to attend the memorial service being held in Great Barrington for Amanda. Jonathan was unable to go because he was scheduled to teach that day, and he had already been reprimanded by his department chairman for neglecting to get grades in on time and failing to meet with students in a timely fashion. Since I hadn't taken so much as a sick day in the last five years, I had no compunction about taking a day off to attend the service, and I thought it might be diplomatic to show some regret at Amanda's untimely passing.

I drove down to the Episcopal Church in Great Barrington on a splendid day in very late October. It had been a slow fall, and the colorful leaves still clung to the branches as if determined to prove that this was what New England was all about. As I walked up to the front of the substantial stone church, I felt that on this day, and in this place, one could almost feel assured that there was indeed a God. I've never been inclined to spend much time thinking about questions that can't be answered. Speculations about the ultimate meaning of things and what happens after death are fruitless in my opinion because there can never be enough evidence in this life to know the answers. Oh, lots of folks believe they know the truth about such things, but to me that's just opinion on steroids. It may make you feel stronger, but in the long run, it's bad for your mental health. But, as I said, today I had a moment of serenity as I walked up to the mahogany doors of the church that I would enjoy until my skeptical sanity returned.

When I entered the sanctuary, I was surprised to see how many people were there. I was forced to sit three-quarters of the way back from the altar due to crowd. I had just slid in on the aisle end, leaving a space next to me, when I heard a voice say, "Is there room for me?"

I turned and saw Lynn Samson waddling toward me. She was wearing black slacks which only served to emphasize her broad beam, a white blouse with a peculiar tie at the neck, and a hat that looked like a crushed fedora. All I could think of was an awkward, over-sized matador who could easily be gored by even the most nearsighted of bulls.

"Of course there's room," I said, edging over and smiling.

"I was afraid there wouldn't be anyone here that I knew," she said, settling down on the pew and bringing her rear over far enough to make contact with mine. I tried to edge over a bit more, but I bumped into the woman on the other side of me, who gave me a mutinous look.

"I'm surprised so many people are here," I said. "I didn't think that Amanda knew many in the community."

"I doubt she did, but Harrison Cole was very well regarded in town. He was always generous with his time and money when it came to supporting local charities and projects. Amanda never arranged a service for him when he died, so I think the locals see this service as really being for him more than her."

"I'm surprised that Amanda didn't have a service for her grandfather given that she claimed to adore him so much," I whispered.

"Hmm. She may have adored him, but he didn't adore her. By the terms of his will, he left most of his estate to charity. I'm sure that dampened some of the girl's ardor for her grandfather."

"But she did have the house."

Lynn shook her head until I thought her odd hat would fall off. "The house is on the market. She was simply living there until it sold, and the money was to be disbursed according to the terms of the will."

"But he did give her the power to determine who would carry on his literary legacy, didn't he?"

I may have detected a faint red blush on Lynn's cheeks. "Actually, I may have been a bit misleading on that."

"What do you mean?"

"Well, Harrison's will did not exactly say that Amanda would have any control over who wrote the next Duke Danforth novel. In fact, he named me his literary executor."

"Then why . . .?"

"Amanda threatened to contest the will unless she had a role in determining the future of her grandfather's writing. I thought it would be easiest just to accede to her wishes. Ultimately, the real choice would have been mine anyway."

"Why did she care? Was it a way for her to make money?"

Lynn shook her head. "She had no need for money. Her parents were quite wealthy and gave her whatever she wanted, and when they died together in a car accident three years ago, she inherited a very sizable estate. No, I think she wanted to be involved with her grandfather's writing because it was a way of staying connected to a man she had adored, even though he finally rejected her."

I hadn't thought it possible for me to feel sorry for Amanda but at that moment I did. But I also realized that I was surrounded by a cloud of duplicity coming from several sources: Amanda's lies about her role in her grandfather's legacy, Lynn's failure to tell us the truth about how the writer of future Cole novels would be determined, and most importantly, Jonathan's massaging of the truth by letting me think he hardly knew a famous writer, when the man was virtually a second father to him. The dishonesty surrounding me seemed almost palpable. For a moment I felt slightly faint. How many people who I thought I knew had only a passing acquaintance with the truth? We expect the people we trust to be honest with us. That's why those closest to us are the ones most capable of deceiving us. I didn't think I'd be quite so trusting ever again.

My distress must have showed because Lynn asked me if I was okay.

"Yes, but you do realize that this little scam you concocted with Amanda probably cost the girl her life," I said bluntly, wanting to hurt.

Lynn appeared startled. "Do you really think someone killed her because of Harrison's novels?"

"I don't know. But she wouldn't have been up here in her grandfather's house if you had told her to get lost when she came around trying to insinuate herself into his will."

"Perhaps, but we won't know precisely why she was murdered unless and until the police come up with a likely suspect. It may turn out to have had nothing to do with the Cole novels. She wasn't a mentally well girl and her problems manifested in a way that made her enemies."

"In what ways specifically?" I asked.

"The usual ways of the young. Stealing other girls' boyfriends, breaking up marriages, spreading malicious gossip, preventing people she knew from getting what they wanted. I'm quite sure she had plenty of enemies down in the city."

"She must have had some friends," I said, glancing around the church, as if I could somehow identify a friend of Amanda's.

"She had drinking and snorting companions more than friends, and I suspect many of them only tolerated her because she was free with her money. In fact, the only person who is likely to have cared for her just walked up the aisle."

I glanced up the side aisle and saw a tall, slender man in his late thirties wearing a nice suit walk up to the front of the church and take a seat on the first pew.

"Who's he?" I asked.

"Ross Kennedy. He was Amanda's fiancé."

Amanda had been engaged and still tried to seduce my husband, I thought, feeling shocked. Clearly, I didn't get out enough in the wrong circles. Living in the country for too long had made me naive.

"He was also her psychologist," Lynn said.

"Aren't there ethics rules about that sort of thing?"

Lynn chortled. "He wasn't actually her psychologist but that's what he does for a living. He's quite an up and comer in the city with a rather exclusive practice. Harrison talked to me about it once. Apparently, Amanda and Ross met at a party for rich young things and were attracted to each other. Nature took its course, but Ross quickly recognized that Amanda had serious problems. However, instead of abandoning her, he tried to help her weather the ups and downs of her condition and became her de facto shrink."

"His behavior sounds a bit borderline."

"In my experience, most men who become shrinks need one."

A man in clerical vestments stood on the alter and the service began. Although I'm not a churchgoer, everything seemed to follow the pattern I was familiar with from television and the movies. Uplifting passages from the scriptures were read, hymns were sung, and the clergyman said a few words about Amanda's brief life. Not having been acquainted with her, his comments lacked something in detail, and knowing his audience, he said rather more than necessary about what a fine man her grandfather had been. Finally, he introduced Ross Kennedy to give the eulogy.

Kennedy was a handsome man with wavy black hair. He stood with the grace and confidence of someone who knew he was respected and considered it his rightful due. His voice was deep, and even reading a grocery list would have been mesmerizing. I was sure his female patients were in no hurry to be cured. A forty-five-minute hour with him might well be the highlight of their week. But as I focused on what he was saying, it became clear to me that he was attempting to give a balanced portrait of a troubled young woman. For every positive trait he mentioned, he offset it with a less than complimentary example taken from her life. There was something bracing and refreshing about his desire for accuracy, but I was pretty sure that when my time came, I would prefer that my eulogist breeze over the negative and dwell on the positive. After all, a eulogy was supposed to be more of a sales pitch for a person's life than an objective evaluation. I saw people glancing sideways at each other as if wondering whether this was a eulogy or a case study.

When Kennedy was done and had returned to his seat, another hymn was sung and then a benediction given. As the crowd streamed out of the back of the church, I walked along with Lynn, keeping to her slow pace. We stopped for a moment in front of the church, while she did some readjustment of her outfit.

"When do you go back to New York?" I asked.

"Sunday. I have friends who have summer homes up here. I'm getting together with some of them and making a weekend of it."

"Nice. I want to tell you that I very much appreciate your willingness to keep Jonathan on the Duke Danforth project. It's meant a lot to him at a difficult time." I kept it vague, not wanting to let her know the police suspicions.

"I understand. Some of my friends have high-placed contacts in town. So, I understand why your husband may be feeling some pressure." Suddenly her eyes bored into mine. "Did he kill Amanda?"

"Of course not," I replied automatically. Then I spoke more slowly, wanting to be very convincing. "Jonathan may be a lot of things but he's not a cold-blooded killer. If Amanda had been pushed in the heat of an argument and hit her head on the edge of a piece of furniture and died, I'd be less certain about Jonathan's innocence, but I found her body and she had been battered to death without mercy. Jonathan simply isn't capable of that level of brutality."

Lynn nodded slowly. "I'm inclined to agree. But in the final event, it doesn't matter what you think or what I think. The opinion of the police is what matters. If Jonathan is arrested for Amanda's murder, there is no way that Harrison Cole's publishers are going to accept him as the new author of the Danforth books. Readers and other members of the publishing community would be up in arms. Under those circumstances, I'd have to look for someone else to take on the job."

"I understand, and I hope it never comes to that," I replied.

"So do I," Lynn said. "So do I."

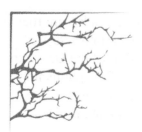

Chapter Eleven

The next day was Saturday. That's when the police returned.

We were both in the kitchen finishing our breakfast when the doorbell rang. Jonathan was already standing, so he went to answer it. I stood in the hallway behind him, curious as to who would be calling on us early on a Saturday morning. When the door opened, Lieutenant Cranston was standing there looking as inelegant as ever. He shoved a piece of paper into Jonathan's hands.

"This entitles us to search your house and grounds. You can read it at your leisure. We'd appreciate it if you and our wife would move into the living room and not impede the officers in any way."

He stepped into the hall and four uniformed police came rushing in behind him. One headed down the hallway toward me, while two went upstairs. Cranston directed us into the living room, and we took our usual seats. A young policewoman came into the room to join us. She sat on the straight-backed, wooden chair. I figured her job was to make certain that we didn't try to conceal any evidence during the search.

"What's this all about?" Jonathan said to her in a querulous tone.

"We are executing a search warrant," she said primly.

"But for what?"

She stared into the distance and didn't reply. But I did notice her glance drifted back to Jonathan's face when he wasn't looking. Most women found him hard not to notice. I could hear heavy footsteps going through all the rooms upstairs. First, they went through our bedroom, then the bathroom, and finally into Jonathan's study. I could hear cabinet doors being opened and closed in the kitchen. Drawers were being pulled out and utensils being rifled through. The man then left the kitchen and after a quick glance through the downstairs half bath, he came into the living room. He began by going through the doors in the end table and got down on his knees to look under all the furniture. He paid particular attention to our fireplace, which we never used.

"What's the meaning of this?" Jonathan asked angrily, but the officer ignored him.

A half hour later when they had completed the search of the house, Lieutenant Cranston came into the living room.

"We noticed that you don't have a fireplace poker," he said, glancing at both of us in turn.

Jonathan just looked sulky and refused to answer. I didn't see much benefit in that.

"That set was there when we moved in. There's never been a poker, just a brush and shovel."

"Don't you find that inconvenient?" he asked.

"No, because we never build a fire. My husband has an allergy to smoke."

He nodded. "May I have the keys to your vehicles. They're included in the search warrant."

Since Jonathan showed no inclination to move, I walked into the kitchen and got our car keys out of the drawer where we usually keep them. I handed them to the lieutenant, and he thanked me.

"I don't know why you're helping these fascists," Jonathan hissed.

I sighed. "Because the sooner they discover that we've got nothing to hide, the sooner they'll leave us alone."

That earned me a contemptuous grunt.

Several minutes later Lieutenant Cranston returned, followed by a uniformed officer who was carrying something in his arms wrapped in plastic.

"Which of you usually drives the black Subaru?" he asked.

"That's my car," Jonathan answered.

"Mine is the dark blue Subaru," I volunteered.

Why Jonathan had purchased a black car was something of a mystery to me. Perhaps he wanted to send the message that cars meant nothing to him or maybe he fantasized that it was one day going to turn into a limousine when he became a wealthy writer.

"Is that the car you used to travel to Amanda Beaumont's home on the day she was murdered?" the lieutenant asked.

"Of course," Jonathan said with ill-disguised impatience.

The officer in uniform stepped forward and without removing the plastic, he held the object close to Jonathan's face.

"Do you recognize this item?" Cranston asked.

"It appears to be a fireplace poker."

"Yes. And if we're correct, it's a match to the other implements found by the fireplace in Ms. Beaumont's study. We'll have to have the laboratory analyze it, of course, but it also looks to have blood and hair on the end."

"So, it must be the murder weapon," Jonathan said.

"That's what we think. Do you have any idea how it came to be in the compartment underneath the floor of your trunk?"

Jonathan's mouth opened and closed, but no words came out. He turned to me in a panic.

"I'm sure my husband has no idea how that got there. Someone else must have put it in his trunk. As you can see, we don't have a garage, so our cars are always in the driveway. Sometimes he forgets to lock his, so anyone could have had access to it."

"It would have to be a someone who also had access to the murder weapon. Did you notice if the fireplace poker was still in the study when you found the body?" the lieutenant asked me.

I shook my head. "I didn't look around the room. Once I saw the body, I went outside and called the police."

"So, it could already have been removed from the scene?"

"I suppose."

The lieutenant walked over and asked Jonathan to please stand.

"Jonathan McAdams, I'm arresting you for the murder of Amanda Beaumont."

He then launched into the Miranda warning, which was a blur of meaningless words in my mind.

"Sarah," Jonathan called out as they cuffed him and led him from the room.

"Don't worry. We'll get you the best lawyer around. You'll be out soon."

He looked over his shoulder with fear in his eyes as they led him away.

AN HOUR LATER MY FRONT doorbell rang. I marched down the hall expecting to see that the police had returned. I was in no mood to talk to them, having spent the last hour calling around trying to find a criminal lawyer for Jonathan. I'd started with the attorney who had written our wills, and she referred me on from there. Getting a lawyer on a Saturday is as challenging as getting a physician, probably they're all out playing golf together. But finally, I managed to reach someone who said that he'd get right down to the police station to be with Jonathan. It turned out not to be the police returning, however, but our neighbor Maggie.

"Sorry to bother you," she said, probably noticing the impatient expression on my face. "But I saw the police here earlier, and I wondered if everything is all right."

I gave her a weak smile. There was no point in alienating my one friend in the neighborhood. I had a feeling that once the news of Jonathan's arrest got out, my popularity as a neighbor would plunge.

"C'mon inside," I said, and led her into the living room. We sat next to each other on the sofa.

"I'm afraid that the police have arrested Jonathan," I told her.

"What for?" she asked, genuinely shocked.

"They believe that he murdered Amanda Beaumont. The woman he was working with on the next Duke Danforth novel."

"I read in the paper that she had died under suspicious circumstances, but why would the police even suspect Jonathan?"

"Because he was with her shortly before she was killed. And they'd just had an argument over creative differences." Maggie wasn't a gossip as far as I knew, but I wasn't going to tell her about the girl's attempt to seduce my husband.

Maggie twisted her hands in her lap, obviously agitated. "I'm sure writers get into disagreements all the time, and they don't lead to murder. The police must just be desperate to pin this murder on anyone. Jonathan is certainly no killer."

"I agree."

"Do they have any solid evidence?"

Again, I was reluctant to share with her the discovery of the supposed murder weapon in Jonathan's car. I certainly didn't want that getting spread all around town, convincing people that I was the wife of a crazed killer. Things were going to be tough enough at school when the word of Jonathan's arrest hit the news. I didn't want to add more fuel to the fire.

"I think what they have is circumstantial. Jonathan was at Amanda's house around the time of the murder, and they'd had a disagreement."

"How did the police find out about the argument?" asked Maggie.

"Well, when Jonathan came home and told me about his fight with Amanda and that she was threatening to get him fired from writing the next Harrison Cole novel, I went to talk with her. I thought I could smooth things over between them. Unfortunately, she was already dead when I got there."

"That must have been horrible for you."

"It wasn't a pretty scene. I called the police, and when they arrived, they wanted to know why I was there. I had to tell them the truth."

"Of course you did."

"And once they knew about the argument, they suspected Jonathan."

"Where is Jonathan now?" Maggie asked.

"Down at the police station. I've arranged for a lawyer to meet him there. I only hope he doesn't say anything before his attorney arrives. He sometimes goes on these rants, and he could say something that will hurt his case."

Maggie smiled sympathetically. "I know this is a terrible time for both of you. If there's anything I can do, don't hesitate to let me know. And if you get a chance, fill me in on how things are going with Jonathan."

I promised her that I would, although I intended to be very selective in what I told anyone.

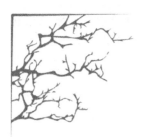

Chapter Twelve

I came home after school the next afternoon having had one of the worst days in my life.

I knew it was going to be a difficult one when I retrieved the morning paper from our front lawn. A rather menacing picture of Jonathan was featured on the front page with a headline story about his arrest for the murder of Harrison Cole's granddaughter. Since Cole had been something of a Berkshire celebrity, the reporter must have thought that he could get some mileage out of stretching the facts available to him into a feature article. I forced myself to read it through carefully and learned nothing new. The majority of the piece was devoted to a summary of Cole's career and a brief, airbrushed summary of Amanda's life.

When I arrived at school and walked down the hall to my classroom, I could tell that most of my colleagues were also newspaper readers. The good morning greetings were more subdued than usual, and several found reasons to look away at the last minute as they passed me. Upon entering the classroom, a sudden silence prevailed. The kind that only occurs when an enthusiastic discussion has been suddenly cut off in mid-sentence. I conducted my classes as usual, without making reference to Jonathan's situation. Aside from a few sniggering comments students made to each other out of my hearing, no one openly raised the subject in class. One of my better students did come up to me after class to say she was sorry that I was going through a difficult time. I was touched that a student could address the matter with more dignity than many of the adults I worked with.

To be fair, one of my closer acquaintances did approach me in the teachers' lounge and express her sympathy, but that was offset by the principal, who sent me a message that he wanted to see me after the school day was over.

"I was very sorry to hear about your situation," Principal Clark said when I was seated in front of his desk like an unruly student. "I just wanted you to know that the superintendent and the chair of the school board understand that this must be a difficult time for you."

I nodded to indicate that it certainly was.

"I was wondering whether you have considered taking any time off to deal with matters. I'm sure much of the burden of this must fall on the spouse."

"I've arranged for a very capable attorney to represent my husband, and I fully expect him to be exonerated in the near future."

The principal cleared his throat. "Of course, that's what we all hope will happen. But until that time, don't you feel that you might be more comfortable not having the daily responsibilities of teaching on top of everything else?"

"To be honest, I think that I'll find coming in to work to be a good distraction from these other concerns. Otherwise, I would just be sitting at home worrying. I think it will also be beneficial to my students to have the continuity of having the same teacher for the entire year."

"There is that to be sure. But the thing is, several parents have already expressed concerns about having their children in close daily contact with someone whose spouse has been accused of such a serious crime."

I stood up and looked down on the plump man behind the too small desk.

"Principal Clark, I believe that by law my husband is innocent until proven guilty, and any attempt by you, the superintendent, or the school board to get me to vacate my tenured position should be carefully considered because I will fight this both legally and in the newspapers. So, you should consider what the potential fallout for all of you might be."

The principal rubbed his hand nervously over his forehead. "It was certainly not my intention to urge you to do anything that you don't wish to do."

"I'm glad to hear that," I said, turning to leave the room. "So, let's not have any further discussion of the matter."

I may have won that battle, but I was certain that this was going to be a war of attrition. The administration in many little ways could make my life miserable in a concerted effort to get me to quit. I knew that I would have to come up with a long-range strategy if I wanted to win the war.

Jonathan's lawyer had told me yesterday afternoon that my husband would be arraigned today. At that time, we would find out what they were charging him with and whether he'd be allowed bail. Not wanting to discuss this on the phone at school, I waited until I got home to call the attorney. His lawyer sounded both harried and forlorn.

"The district attorney is charging Jonathan with second degree murder. In essence, that means they believe that although he did not plan Amanda Beaumont's murder, it was his intention to, in fact, kill her. And I'm afraid that due to the brutality of the attack, the judge has denied your husband bail."

"What does that mean?" I asked.

"He'll be transferred from the local lockup to the Berkshire County jail to await trial."

"And when will that take place?"

"Since the docket is rather full right now, it will probably not be for another three months."

"And he has to sit in jail until then?"

"I'm afraid so."

I took a deep breath. "How is Jonathan holding up?"

"Like most people who aren't hardened criminals, he's not taking it well. He appeared rather distraught. Most men are at first. It takes time for the average guy to get into the swing of things in jail."

I struggled to imagine Jonathan ever getting into that "swing of things." For better or worse, he wasn't the average guy."

"Can he have visitors?" I asked.

"Yes, an inmate in the jail is allowed up to three one-hour visits a week. How about if I arrange for you to see him on Friday? That will give him a few days to get adjusted."

"Fine."

"Okay. I'll give you a call. And, Sarah, please try not to worry too much. We're in the early stages right now. The state has a good case, but it isn't airtight. We still have a chance of winning or at least of getting a deal leading to a reduction in the charge."

I didn't say anything. If his lawyer was already considering doing a deal, things sounded bad for Jonathan.

An hour later, I was out in the kitchen when the phone rang.

"Hi, Sarah, it's Lynn Samson. How are you holding up?"

"Are you still in Great Barrington?" I asked.

"No, I'm back at my office. But a friend from up there just called me with the news that Jonathan has been arrested for Amanda's murder."

"He didn't do it," I said automatically.

Lynn paused. "Remember, I told you that really doesn't matter. The perception of guilt will be enough to keep the publisher from allowing Jonathan to be the new Harrison Cole. I'm afraid that I'm going to have to look for someone else."

"Won't it be hard to start from scratch with someone new?" I asked.

"I thought that Jonathan and Amanda had already completed the first three-quarters of a first draft."

"Jonathan did all of the writing. Amanda simply offered comments and suggestions. And the thing is, since Jonathan was not yet under contract at the time he did that writing, it seems to me that what he's done so far belongs to him and not to you or to any publisher."

"What are you suggesting?" Lynn asked in a hard voice. "Are you going to ask me to pay to get what Jonathan has already written?"

"Not at all. I'm offering you a deal."

"What sort of a deal?"

"I read through Jonathan's first draft last night. It looks pretty good, although there are a few changes I would make to increase tension. He also left some notes on the final quarter which were helpful, but I think I would add a final twist to surprise the reader. My suggestion is that you let me finish the first draft of the novel and see how you like it."

There was a long pause.

"Do you have any writing background?" she asked.

"I took a course in creative writing in college."

A disparaging grunt came down the line. "That's not a positive. How long would it take you to finish the book?"

"In three weeks. I can deliver a polished first draft to you by then."

"And if I don't like it?"

"Then it's yours to take to another writer to whip into shape. Neither Jonathan nor I will have any claims on it. But I'm expecting you to give my submission a fair reading."

"I like you, Sarah. You're a no-nonsense person, unlike most of the writers I deal with every day. I'll promise to give it an honest reading, and if it's usable with normal editing, I'll send it on to the publisher."

"That sounds acceptable."

A chuckle came down the line. "It's been a pleasure doing business with you."

"Same here."

As I hung up, I realized that now all I had to do was write a book. That was hard, but even harder was going to be explaining to Jonathan that I was going to be the author of his novel.

Chapter
Thirteen

The rest of the work week went past in a blur. My students had quickly adjusted to being taught by the wife of an accused felon, and classes were proceeding along normally. One of the things about the young is that they can deal with change and are flexible in their moral judgments. That sometimes gets them into trouble, but often makes them much nicer human beings than their more rigid parents. My colleagues found it harder to adjust. The flow of conversation when I was in the teachers' lounge was still rather stagnant, and people reacted to me with a polite stiffness that hadn't been there before. Perhaps they were afraid that if they offended me, I'd attack them with a fireplace poker. To be honest, the thought had occurred to me on more than one occasion.

When I wasn't at school or preparing lessons on my laptop in the living room at home, I was up in Jonathan's study diligently attempting to complete the next Duke Danforth bestseller. At first, I had felt paralyzed as I stared at the blank page where the story left off. What could I possibly say next? But then I went back and reread the entire book again, this time paying attention to Duke himself as a character. Then the writing started to flow as I realized that I wasn't writing a puzzle to be solved, but a story that grew organically out of Duke's loves, hates, and values. Once I became Duke, the plot opened up to me and the ideas began to follow. After a couple of nights, I was no longer even glancing at Jonathan's notes as I realized on my own what Duke would do next. It was hard for me to be objective, but I felt that I was writing a damned good thriller. But however enthusiastic I might be, I knew that I would have to conceal it on Friday night when I met with Jonathan.

THE ROOM REMINDED ME of every school cafeteria I'd ever eaten in or policed during my teaching career. It had the pervasive smell of dishwasher detergent, cleaning fluid, and generations of barely good-enough meals. It wasn't surprising since due to overcrowding, the jail's visiting room for guests served a dual function as the inmates' cafeteria.

After a quick embrace under the watchful eye of a guard standing by the wall, Jonathan and I sat across from each other on either side of a beige plastic table. He looked as if he had aged ten years. His eyes had dark bags and his shaving had been less than fully accurate, leaving tufts of beard at unexpected spots on his face.

"How are you doing?" I asked.

"How do you think?" he snapped. Then he paused and sighed. "Sorry, I guess things are just getting to me."

"That's only natural but don't give up hope. You'll be out of here before long."

"I'm in here at least for another three months until my trial. Do you know what people are like in here. They're animals."

A big guy at the next table visiting with a woman glanced over, and I motioned for Jonathan to keep his voice down.

"Be careful what you say," I whispered. "Remarks that would have gotten you only a rude response on the outside can get you killed in here."

Jonathan paled but said nothing. His inability to hear himself and calculate the effect of his comments on others had always amazed me. It was as if he believed he had a special dispensation to criticize others without receiving any reaction in return.

"What if I go to trial and get convicted. I'll never make it in prison. I won't survive among these people."

His eyes filled with tears, and I decided it was time to change the subject.

"I heard from Lynn Samson the other day."

"Has she fired me?" he asked with a hangdog expression.

"She wanted to, but I talked her out of it." I paused. I had to express this carefully. "I convinced her to let me finish the novel."

"How did you manage that? You're no writer."

"I told her that using the draft and notes you left behind, I could finish the book. She's willing to look at whatever I submit."

Jonathan gave a malicious smile. "It will be a dog's breakfast. You're a good teacher, Sarah, but you're no writer."

"Well, I guess I'll just do the best I can. At least we're keeping the job in the family for the time being."

He eyed me warily. "Who's going to get credit for the book?"

"We haven't really discussed the details yet. But even if I got the credit, wouldn't that be better than having Lynn find some writer we don't know and see his name on the book."

Jonathan just looked at me, and I knew he found the latter to be preferable. He'd rather be replaced by a professional he didn't know than have me get the credit.

I stood up. "Well, keep your head down and your mouth closed. You may be getting out of here sooner than you think."

"Yeah, yeah," he said. "That's what my lawyer says, too, but I think both of you are full of it."

I left the room thinking that I really didn't need to put up with this abuse. At least his lawyer was getting paid to listen to it.

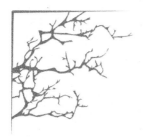

Chapter
Fourteen

I spent the weekend writing as I never had before. Chapter headings zipped by, and the word count dramatically increased. New ideas kept coming to me, and I held in the back of my mind a surprising twist that I wanted to add at the end. Although I knew that I could be writing drivel and be fooling myself into thinking that I was producing solid prose, in my heart of hearts I was confident that what I was writing was good. At least as good as what Jonathan had produced so far and likely even better. When Monday rolled around and I had to return to school instead of spending the day writing, I found that I missed it.

By now I had become hardened to being treated as a virtual pariah by my colleagues and the administration. Principal Clark could barely spare me a grim nod when he passed me in the hall, and only a few of the younger faculty engaged me in casual conversation. I guess it's true that adversity helps us to discover who our true friends are, and apparently mine were very few in number. When I got home on Monday afternoon, I was happy to get into comfortable clothes and prepare myself to sit down and write. The world of Duke Danforth had become much preferable to my own. So, when the doorbell rang, I cursed under my breath as I went to answer it.

When I pulled open the door, a handsome, well-dressed man a bit older than myself stood on the porch. He looked familiar, but it took a moment for the face to register.

"You're . . ."

"Ross Kennedy," he said with a smile, putting out his hand. "I believe that I spotted you at Amanda's memorial service."

I stood there trying to figure out what he wanted.

"May I come in?" he asked.

I couldn't think of a way to refuse that wouldn't make me seem ungracious, so I took him into the living room. He settled into Jonathan's easy chair, which somehow seemed appropriate, while I perched on the edge of the sofa.

"How can I help you?" I asked.

He casually crossed one leg over the other, resting his ankle on his knee and glanced around the room as if he were considering whether to purchase the house.

"I thought it only right that I should inform you personally that I have joined your husband's defense team."

"I didn't know you were a lawyer."

He smiled. "I'm not, but I've done some forensic psychology. Do you know what that is?"

I knew from television that it had something to do with a psychologist who evaluates criminals and said so.

"That's right. Very good of you to know that. I've occasionally testified in court on the fitness of a defendant to stand trial and on his ability to know the difference between right and wrong.

"Do you think that Jonathan may not be fit to stand trial for some reason?"

He shook his head. "No. He is of sound mind and clearly can grasp the significance of what's happening. My involvement here is based more on the fact that I consider him incapable of carrying out an act as brutal as the murder of Amanda."

"I agree with you, but I've known him for over a decade. What do you base your conclusion on?" I didn't like this smooth, smug man who gave the impression that he was doing me a great favor by taking up Jonathan's cause.

"I've had the opportunity to talk with him twice. Once was today at the jail with his lawyer. We spent an hour together, so I can't say that we had an in-depth interview. But it did serve to confirm what I thought from the first time I met him."

"And when was that?"

"A couple of weeks ago. I was visiting Amanda and staying at the same hotel. One afternoon I dropped by to say hello, and your husband was there working. We had a brief conversation."

"I see." Here was another tidbit of information that Jonathan had failed to pass on to me. That Amanda had a fiancé, and he had met him. "And what is your professional opinion of my husband."

"I don't have the liberty to say in any detail given professional standards. However, he is essentially a passive man with a weak ego, and far more likely to

113

retreat than to attack in the face of conflict. His account of what he did after his argument with Amanda seems to be quite in character. I can't imagine him using force except to defend himself, and certainly not to the degree that her injuries indicate."

"Aren't you bothered by the fact that your fiancé tried to seduce my husband?"

He smiled, completely unflustered. "Amanda was always a law unto herself. She didn't feel hemmed in by society's conventions."

"I'd have said she was mentally ill."

Kennedy shrugged. "Again, another conventional generalization. Indeed, Amanda had her issues, and some of them repeatedly got her into difficulties. We were working on them together, and she had been making progress. If we'd had a few more years together, I think her feet would finally have been solidly on the ground."

"Then it's a shame she died when she did. But if you're convinced that my husband didn't kill her, then who do you think did?"

He gave me an insincere smile. "I think we both know the answer to that. You did, of course."

I felt a tightening in my chest and took a deep breath. "The police have thoroughly investigated my account of my actions that evening, and they seem to have no problem with my version of events."

"We both know that as soon as the police found that bloody fireplace poker in your husband's trunk, they stopped any further investigation. It's my contention that you took it from the scene of the crime and placed it there to incriminate your husband."

"And why would I do that?"

"One of the oldest of human emotions—jealousy. You've suspected that your husband was having an affair with Amanda from the first time they started working together. Amanda informed me of your unconvincing performance with the apple pie. As they worked together ever more closely, I think the pressure on you mounted until you confronted Amanda and beat her head in. Then to fully satisfy your desire for revenge, you made it appear that your husband was the killer."

I took several deep breaths to slow my heart rate. "That's a fascinating story, and it certainly makes me out to be quite the monster. When did I have time to do all this?"

He smiled. "That is the issue, isn't it. I've read the police report. You say you left your friends at four o'clock and headed home, arriving there at four-thirty. You claim to have remained there until your husband arrived at seven o'clock. Then, after hearing his story of his argument with Amanda, you left at seven-thirty, arriving back at Amanda's cottage at approximately eight o'clock."

"After Amanda had been murdered."

"But it is my contention that you were not home from four-thirty to seven. You may have returned home at four-thirty, but you left shortly thereafter, once again to spy on your husband and Amanda. Perhaps you even lurked outside the cottage and heard their argument, which would have infuriated you even more. Possibly, your husband was even tempted by Amanda's blandishments until, for some reason, he changed his mind at the last minute. In any event, once your husband left, you entered the cabin and killed Amanda. You left, taking the fireplace poker with you, which you later secreted in your husband's car to deflect guilt from yourself."

"That's a fascinating story, but there's not a word of truth in it. And I doubt very much that you can find any evidence to corroborate it."

"We'll see. But that will be my working hypothesis, which it never was for the police. And one's hypothesis tends to determine what one sees. I'm going to begin by canvassing your neighborhood to discover if anyone spotted your car leaving the street between four-thirty and five-thirty. If I can find a witness to that, it will certainly support an alternate version of events that will help free your husband and possibly put you in jail in his place."

"Would you like me to take you around and introduce you to my neighbors right now?" I offered, hoping my bravado would indicate my innocence.

He smiled. "Sadly, I have to return to the city for a couple of days to catch up with my patients, but I will be back soon to continue my investigations."

He got to his feet, straightened the crease in his pants, and headed for the door. I followed along, not sure what to say next. He stopped in the doorway.

"I think you will prove to be a very determined adversary," he said, smiling. "I look forward to this investigation."

I shook my head. "I'm not your adversary."

"Of course you would say that. But I know differently."

I stood in the doorway while he went down the walk to his car. As he drove away, I looked over toward Maggie's. She was raking the leaves under her red maple tree. She often said that if it wasn't so beautiful much of the year, she'd have it taken out because of all the mess it produced. She saw me standing there and waved. A minute later she walked over.

"Who was that hunk?" she asked.

"Ross Kennedy. He was Amanda Beaumont's fiancé."

"Bit of an age difference there." Maggie shrugged. "But I guess nobody cares about that sort of thing anymore. Even so, a good-looking man."

"He's a psychologist."

"Ugh! Keep him away from me, then. I don't want any man around me who can read my thoughts."

"Well, you may be meeting him whether you like it or not. A couple of days from now, he's going to be going door-to-door to see if anyone spotted my car leave the house between four-thirty and six on the evening Amanda was killed."

Maggie frowned. "Why would he care about that?"

"He believes that I killed her."

"Then he's a fool as well as a psychologist."

I smiled at Maggie in her baggy, mismatched sweats. "I hope that's what the police think when he presents his theory."

I went inside and slumped down on the sofa in the living room. I knew that I hadn't killed Amanda, but when Kennedy was telling me his theory, I could almost imagine it to be true. His hypothesis held

117

together and made sense. I didn't think the police would buy it unless he had more evidence, but if one of my neighbors said that they thought they had seen me leave during the time in question, it might be enough to give credence to what he was claiming. I hadn't gone out in that time frame, but who knows what someone might say if Kennedy prodded their memories enough. I could see him easily being able to sway people with his sonorous voice. I remembered reading somewhere that eyewitness accounts are often the least reliable because people often imagine that they saw things they didn't because they want to be helpful to the person questioning them.

I agreed with Kennedy that Jonathan was a very unlikely killer, but I knew that I hadn't done it. What suspects were left? Suddenly, it occurred to me that everything Kennedy had said about my motivation for killing Amanda also applied to him. It was his fiancé who was trying to seduce my husband. What if he hadn't been as cool with that as he let on? Maybe he'd finally gotten tired of her promiscuous ways and decided to put an end to her. He knew where she lived, and he could have hidden outside the cottage as easily as I. He was also a big, strong guy capable of overpowering her without difficulty. He also might have known where Jonathan and I lived and come by at night to put the poker in Jonathan's trunk. After all, as I'd told the police, we had no garage, and Jonathan frequently left his car unlocked.

I suddenly felt better. If Kennedy went to the police with his version of events, I could present a story of my own that would be at least equally as convincing. Maybe the result would be to leave the police uncertain as to who the real culprit was. That might be bad for the course of justice but at least it would get Jonathan out of jail. With that happy thought in mind, I headed upstairs. It was time to write if I was going to meet Lynn's deadline. Whether Jonathan was pleased about it or not, I was now responsible for producing the next Duke Danforth novel.

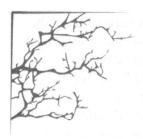

Chapter Fifteen

I was walking into school the next morning when Principal Clark rushed out of his office.

"I'd like to speak with you in my office for a moment, Sarah," he said in a firm voice.

I glanced at my watch. "I have to be in class in ten minutes."

"This won't take long."

I followed him into his office and remained standing as he walked behind his desk, probably for protection.

"I want you to have your lesson plans for next week on my desk by Friday," he said without meeting my eye.

"Why? You normally only ask that of first-year teachers."

"Under the circumstances, I thought it necessary to make certain that you are able to keep up with your responsibilities."

"Have there been any complaints that I haven't been?"

"Not as of yet."

"Well then, I would suggest that we wait until there are before you hold me to a different standard than other tenured teachers."

"This is not a request. I am ordering you to have those plans to me by Friday."

"No. And if my refusal leads to your taking any disciplinary action, I can assure you that I will have a human rights lawyer looking into the practices in this school. So go back and tell the superintendent or the chairman of the board or whoever is pulling your strings that if they want a fight, they will certainly get one. And I can guarantee that they won't be pleased with the outcome."

Clark puffed out his cheeks as I turned and marched out of his office.

I was still fuming when I entered the classroom, and I had to take several deep breaths that I released slowly before calming down. I wanted to be careful not to take my anger at the administration out on the students, who in my opinion were more capable of running the place than the current management. Once I got into teaching my lessons, my mind gradually returned to an even keel. I'd just have to see how much legal risk the administration was willing to take to be rid of someone who had become an embarrassment to them. I suspected not a lot. Most teachers who go into administration are not willing to be heroes. If they were, they'd stay in the classroom. Mostly, they're full of threat and bluster and accustomed to browbeating students or the more docile faculty. Like most bullies, if you stand up to them, you can get them to back off. I'd just have to see how this played out. If Jonathan got convicted, it could get dicey.

When I came home that afternoon, I was tired both from teaching and the emotional trauma of my confrontation with Clark. I rushed upstairs and got out of my teaching clothes and into a comfortable sweater and jeans. I hadn't had much lunch because things were rather frosty in the teachers' cafeteria. Whenever I sat down at a table, the conversation became polite to the point of being stilted, so I had taken to bringing my lunch and eating in a corner in the lounge and reading a book. At the moment, a book was a better companion that a fellow teacher. I was focusing on thrillers, thinking it might be a good idea to read a few if I was going to write one. As a result, I was hungry when I got home, and after changing, I rushed into the kitchen for a snack.

That was when I noticed that the back door stood open. Now, Jonathan was notorious for leaving doors and windows unlocked. I sometimes thought he did it on purpose as a sign that his mind was on higher things than personal security. But I am generally very careful about such matters, and I was certain that the back door had been locked when I left for school. Since I had already been through most of the house, I was pretty sure there was no intruder still there, but then I thought of the basement, a dank place where I only went to do the weekly laundry. I walked down the hall to the umbrella stand and pulled out the cane that Jonathan had used when he'd broken an ankle the one time he'd tried hiking. It wasn't very heavy but better than nothing.

I made my way back to the kitchen and opened the door to the cellar. Slowly, I made my way down the creaky stairs, being as quiet as possible. I might have announced my presence if an intruder had another avenue of escape so I could avoid a confrontation. But the exterior hatch out of the cellar was rusted closed. If some deranged killer wanted to escape, he'd have to go through me.

As soon as I reached the bottom of the stairs, I turned on the switch that lit up a series of bare bulbs strung across the basement. Even though the light was rather dim, I could see clearly from one end of the cellar to the other. No one was there. I paused a moment to take stock of the situation. Assuming someone had broken in and I hadn't accidentally left the door open, what would their purpose have been. If they'd wanted to take something, it wasn't obvious what it could be. I'd already been through the upstairs enough to know that Jonathan's computer and the television in the living room were still there. We kept hardly any cash in the house, and my costume jewelry could be replaced for a couple of hundred dollars.

Perhaps someone had broken in not to take something but to leave something. Perhaps an item that would incriminate me in Amanda's murder. I could easily imagine Ross Kennedy doing that since he seemed to have a vendetta against me. I surveyed the basement looking for anything I didn't recognize. Basically, all that was down there were some boxes with surplus household goods, which by the layer of undisturbed dust on the surface hadn't been recently opened, two suitcases for the few times we traveled anywhere, and a small workbench left by the previous

123

owner where the modest collection of tools we owned were haphazardly scattered. As far as I could tell, there were no new incriminating additions.

I went back upstairs and searched through the rooms and closets. Aside from finding a few things that had been missing for a while, nothing surprising came to light. As I stood in the kitchen, taking a last glance around, it occurred to me to examine the door to see how an intruder might have gotten in. I examined the door itself and the frame. Everything seemed to be as it always was. Then it occurred to me to check on the window over the sink. Before I even reached it, I could see that it was unlocked. Jonathan frequently complained about the heat in the kitchen when I cooked and often opened that window. He usually forgot to lock it again, and sometimes I did as well. I raised the window, and it went up easily. The window was easily reached from our back porch, and although the opening wasn't large, an agile person of average size could probably work their way inside. It would be harder to get out again that way because of the location of the sink.

The more I thought about it, the more I considered it likely that the intruder had come in through the window, then unlocked the back door and left that way. But why? A bad thought came to me, and I rushed upstairs to turn on Jonathan's computer. I breathed a sigh of relief when the file containing the new Danforth book came up just as I had left it. I realized that this was truly the most valuable thing in the house. I fumbled around in Jonathan's desk until I found a flash drive that had enough space on it, and I downloaded the manuscript to it. I'd make a practice of updating it after each writing session and hiding in one of my shoes in the closet. I couldn't imagine who would want to steal it, but the way life had been going recently, I didn't trust anyone.

Since I was already in front of the computer, I sat down to work on the book for a while. When I next looked up it had gotten dark, and the clock read six. I went into my bedroom and pulled my laptop out of the bag I used to carry it to school. I went downstairs and discovered that I was ravenous, not having had my snack. I made a large bowl of pasta and ate it in front of the television as I watched the news, sitting in Jonathan's easy chair. I spent another half hour updating my lesson plans, just in case Clark came around with armed guards to wrest them from me tomorrow.

Even though I was feeling quite tired, I knew that I had to return to the study and work some more on the novel. I was making good progress, but I wanted to have the first draft out to Lynn by Friday. I felt some nervous tension in my chest at the thought that she might not like it, and all my efforts would have been for nothing. I didn't think that would be the case, but I had learned from Jonathan's experiences at trying to get published that there was no way to predict the preferences of agents or editors.

Suppressing a sigh, I headed upstairs to get back to the writing, knowing that in a few moments I would no longer feel tired as I entered into the exciting world of Duke Danforth. I had gotten upstairs before I remembered that I wanted to strengthen the lock on the back kitchen window by putting in longer screws. As I started back downstairs,

I tripped on the top step and had to reach out desperately to grab the banister to right myself. That had happened several times in the past month, and every time I had told myself that I should tack down the raised area of carpet before there was an accident. It was my responsibility. Just as Jonathan avoided housework, he was also oblivious to home repairs. On some level, he must have thought that an angel came into the house while we were asleep at night to do those chores. The angel, of course, was me. Knowing how his mother had doted on him, I could see where his blindness to domestic duties came from.

I went down into the basement again to get a screwdriver and see if we had some long screws. I managed to find both, and while I was down there, I looked for a hammer to fix the carpet. I poked around for several minutes without success. I knew we had one, but it could easily have been left at the sight of its last usage. I sometimes wasn't good at returning tools to the basement. I decided that I'd focus on the window for tonight, and just be careful on the stairway until the hammer surfaced.

Feeling more secure, once the kitchen window was firmly locked in place, I went back upstairs and lost myself in a world of suspense and adventure. It was midnight before I stopped, and I went to bed and slept as soundly as I ever had. Duke was turning out to be a good companion.

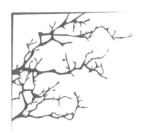

Chapter Sixteen

I came home Thursday afternoon filled with anticipation. School had gone along smoothly since Monday. Clark had now taken to walking past me in the halls as if I were invisible. I considered that a good sign that fear had won out over his desire to be done with me. More importantly, the writing had been going extremely well. The first draft was completely finished and in a polished state. I was going to spend the evening going over it one more time before sending it out to Lynn tomorrow morning. I wanted her to see it the first thing when she came in Friday morning. I had read that you should let your manuscript sit for several days then read it one more time before submission, but I considered it more important that I prove to Lynn that I could work to a tight deadline. I didn't want to give her any excuse to think that she should turn the job over to another writer.

As I was heading downstairs to get a bottle of water to bring up to the study, I tripped once again on the raised carpet at the top of the stairs. This was getting to be a real health risk, and I found that I had an unusually strong desire to survive long enough to get the book out to the publisher. I felt like an expectant mother being anxious to take care of herself in order to guarantee the life of her child. So, I headed down to the basement, determined to do a thorough search for the hammer that I knew had to be there.

Just as I did last night, I went into the cellar and put on all the lights. But unlike last night, as I approached the workbench I could see, lying there front and center, a claw hammer. I drew closer. It was impossible that I could have missed this in my search last night. I picked up the hammer, and immediately noticed that the end was covered with what appeared to be blood and hair. I paused for a moment, disgusted by what I was seeing. How had this gotten here and what had it been used for?

I leaned against the workbench and thought hard. The only theory that made sense was that someone had broken into my house yesterday in order to steal my hammer. They then had used the hammer for something that was likely wrong if not illegal. Then they had broken in again today and returned the hammer to a spot where it would easily be found.

That told me one thing. I had to get rid of this hammer as soon as possible because whoever had stolen it was using it to set me up for a crime. I went upstairs wondering how someone could have gotten into the house a second time. I checked the window over the sink. It was closed and securely locked. The backdoor had been closed and locked when I came back from school today. So, the person who had gotten in had used a different method of entry. I slumped down at the kitchen table and reviewed the possibilities. My eyes drifted to the wall across from me. I saw the hook on the wall where the extra key to the backdoor was usually kept. The hook was empty. The person who had broken in yesterday had taken the spare key.

That meant someone was out there with a key to my backdoor, and he could come and go at whim. That was a problem I'd have to deal with quickly. I could have all the locks changed tomorrow, but there was no way I'd be able to go to sleep in the house tonight without having that door secured in some fashion. But before I dealt with that, I had to dispose of the hammer. It stared at me like a one-eyed, red monster from the kitchen counter. At any moment, the police could arrive to search the house, and they'd find me with a hammer covered in blood. Not a good look, especially for the wife of an accused killer.

I went back down in the basement. Fortunately, when we'd moved into the house three years ago, I'd purchased new bushes for the front of the house and put them in myself. That meant that I did have a shovel. I brought the shovel up to the kitchen and considered the best plan of attack.

I decided to have something to eat while I waited for it to get dark. Three hours later, I thought it was time to get to work. The nearest streetlamp was about twenty yards away at the end of the street, so very little light reached any part of the backyard. If I walked forty yards from the back of the house, I'd be in complete darkness. I went upstairs and put on a dark blue hoodie. Turning the lights out in the kitchen, I began walking directly back, away from the house, carrying the shovel and the hammer.

I chose a spot and glanced up and down the backyards. There were no neighbors to the left of us, but on the right was Maggie's house. I could see a light on in the living room and in one of the upstairs bedrooms. No one would be able to see me, but I was concerned that in this quiet neighborhood, they might hear the shoveling. I'd just have to hope that with two young children, any sounds I made would go unnoticed.

Being as careful as possible to neatly remove the turf in one piece, I began to dig. Fortunately, we'd had rain the day before and the ground was moist. It made the digging easier. Working quietly and carefully, in less than half an hour I had a two-foot-deep hole dug that would hold the hammer. I gingerly dropped it into the darkness, and began to refill the hole, carefully packing the dirt down as I went along. When the hole was filled in, I carefully replaced the turf. It was difficult to tell in the dark, but I hoped it looked as natural as possible. A soft rain had begun to fall, and I figured that it might cover up some of the disruption of the soil that I had caused. It would have to do. I couldn't afford to check on it in the daytime. I didn't want any neighbor to be able to tell that they spotted me surveying the ground in my backyard.

I carried the shovel back into house. I washed it off in the sink and carefully dried it with paper towels that I immediately put out in the garbage. The next problem was securing the back door. By putting my weight into it, I was able to slide the kitchen table across the laminate floor and shove it up against the door. I then went to the recycle bin and got out some empty cans which I place along the edge of the table.

Someone strong might be able to push the door open but not without creating a racket. I planned to sleep on the sofa in the living room with the cane beside me. Maybe I wouldn't get much sleep, but I'd be ready for any intruder.

Feeling pretty good about what I had accomplished, I took the cane and went up to the study. With the door remaining open, I could easily hear if someone tried to break into the house. I settled down and began working on the final review of the manuscript. Although a little distracted at first, after a while I settled into my work, and three hours later I was well satisfied with my first Duke Danforth novel. It was finally ready to send off to Lynn Samson in the morning.

I decided to sleep in my clothes in case I had to repel boarders, so taking the cane with me, I settled in down on the sofa. I thought that I might lie awake for hours feeling anxious, but there's apparently nothing like writing to make you tired enough to sleep. I was out almost instantly. I awoke a few times in the night because the sofa made a rather poor bed, but once I got oriented and realized where I was, I quickly went back to sleep again.

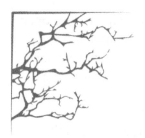

Chapter
Seventeen

The next morning, I got to school feeling pleased with myself. I had emailed the file containing my manuscript to Lynn first thing in the morning. Now came the waiting. I knew it was unlikely that I'd hear from her before Monday at the earliest, but I was on tenterhooks wanting to know her decision. I'd gone through this sort of waiting many times in the past with Jonathan and had often pointed out to him that he should be more patient. Now I realized that wanting to know the future of something you have spent hours of work, skill, and love crafting made patient waiting an impossibility. At least I had teaching as a distraction. Sitting at home listening for the phone would have made the tension unbearable.

During my break, I had called a locksmith and arranged to meet him at home in the afternoon to change my locks. I found myself during idle moments wondering who had broken into my house and what significance the bloody hammer had. I suspected that it would all be made clear to me sooner rather than later. Another complication that I didn't need in my life right now.

The locksmith's van pulled up in front of my house just as I parked my car in the driveway. I explained that I wanted the locks on both doors changed. I'd decided to be safe rather than sorry and have both done. He showed me a couple of options, and we decided on one that seemed of good quality yet wouldn't break the bank. I left him preparing to work and went upstairs to change out of my school clothes. No sooner had I gotten into a flannel shirt and jeans than the phone rang.

"Can you talk for a few minutes?" Lynn Samson said abruptly when I answered.

"Sure." By the tone of her voice I was certain that she hadn't liked my story and was going to tell me that she planned to hire a professional writer to take over the project.

"Of course, I'll have to run it by the publisher," she said. "But this appears to be perfectly acceptable as the next Duke Danforth thriller."

"Really?"

"The plotting is solid and your writing leaps off the page. You've got a wonderful flair for the dramatic scene, and even on a fast reading, I can see flashes of wit and insight that Harrison himself would have been proud to produce."

"Thanks," I said, feeling breathless.

"And the improvements you made on the draft that Jonathan produced are very impressive."

"Wait. How did you get to see Jonathan's draft? I thought I had the only copy."

"One of Amanda's last acts was to send me a file with everything Jonathan had written so far."

"So, if I really didn't have anything to bargain with, why did you agree to make a deal with me to write the rest of the novel?"

A short laugh came down the phone. "Because I like you, and in our brief conversations I saw someone who is a keen observer of life. I was willing to negotiate with the publisher to extend the deadline for a few more days in order to see what you could do. And I haven't been disappointed."

"You really thought that I improved on Jonathan's work?"

"To be honest with you, his work is adequate but rather pedestrian. He does the things you would expect of someone whose taken all the right workshops and gotten the degrees, but you have a way of approaching a story sideways which intrigues and baffles the reader. You have an unusual mind. That's a special talent required to write a thriller. No, this book isn't Jonathan's. It's all yours. We don't want Jonathan associated with it in any way. And that raises the question of what name you should write under."

"What's wrong with my name?" I asked.

"If Jonathan is tried for the murder of Amanda Beaumont, the name of McAdams is going to be headline news for a while. The publisher won't be happy having the new Harrison Cole identified as the spouse of the killer of his granddaughter. Some of his fans simply won't buy the book for that reason alone, and no matter how much good publicity the book gets, that will be a constant cloud hanging over it. No, you need to write under a pen name, and we'll keep it under wraps for a while as to who you really are. Once you're established writing the Danforth books and have an audience, it won't matter. You could personally kill Bambi and your books would still sell. But up until then, we need to keep you under cover, so to speak."

I thought for a moment. "My family name is Lane. What if I write as Sarah Lane?"

"Wonderful. It's a good, simple American name. Short enough to be easily remembered."

"Will the contract be in that name?"

"No. That will be in your legal name, but the publisher will keep that a secret. We'll do the same thing for the next book. After that, we'll have to see what the situation is like."

"The next book?" I asked, feeling both excited and frightened.

"Of course. Remember what I said about wash, rinse, and repeat. Publishers are very conservative. Once they've found someone who can produce a good product on time, they aren't going to want to lose her. I expect that along with this book, they'll give you a contract for two more with an advance on the next."

"Will there be a lot of money?"

"Probably your advance will be more than you make in a couple of years of teaching. And if they like the next book you submit, we can negotiate for an even bigger advance. Of course, that's assuming you want me to represent you."

"I'd like that very much."

"Good. I'll send you a contract later today. I look forward to our having a long and profitable relationship."

"As do I."

"How are things going with Jonathan?" she asked in a more somber tone.

"He's still in the county jail awaiting trial. It's not clear that they have enough evidence to convict him, but the state is apparently pressing on with the case."

"That's a shame. I find it very hard to believe that he had anything to do with Amanda's death. She was a young woman who made enemies simply by breathing. You'd think there would be a host of other suspects for the police to investigate."

"Unfortunately, he had motive, means, and opportunity. For the police, that's the trifecta."

"Well, we can only hope that someone else comes under suspicion."

"Right." As long as that someone wasn't me.

After I hung up, I went downstairs and read in the living room while the locksmith finished his work. Once he had handed me several sets of keys and again told me the benefits of the fine locks he had installed, I paid him. I took comfort in knowing that I'd at least be able to sleep in my bedroom tonight.

I went into the kitchen and put a frozen dinner in the microwave. I found that I had less and less interest in preparing meals now that I was eating by myself. One thing Jonathan had provided me with was a dining companion who had a healthy appetite.

When the microwave pinged, I debated with myself whether to have a celebratory glass of wine with my meal, even though I rarely indulged. I was going to be a published author, that made it a special occasion. The idea lit up in my mind like a neon sign. I felt like singing, dancing, and laughing all at the same time. Even if my identity had to be kept a secret, I'd know what I had accomplished, and sometimes the most pleasant experiences are the ones we share quietly and only with ourselves. This was a feeling I wanted to dwell on in solitude for a while. Opening it up to others would somehow diminish it.

The biggest problem was going to be how to keep the news from Jonathan. Finding out that I had gotten the contract for the book that he expected to receive credit for would plunge him even further into despair. And the fact that I had replaced him would be a final insult that his always fragile ego would never recover from. He'd see me as a traitor who had stolen his work. Was I? I knew that the changes I'd made to his draft were so substantial that it had become a different book, and the last quarter I had written completely on my own. But I'd try to make it up to him anyway by splitting the royalties for that book with him. Unfortunately, there was no way to split the fame, and he'd never forgive me for that.

I was contemplating that dark thought when the police came.

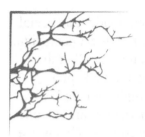

Chapter
Eighteen

Lieutenant Cranston stood on the front porch looking even more disheveled than I remembered. His sergeant and an officer in uniform were lined up in a row behind him. I wondered if he'd brought reinforcements because I was about to be arrested.

"May I speak with you for a few minutes?" Cranston requested, pulling ineffectually at the wrinkles in his none-too-clean raincoat.

Silently, I led them into the living room, making certain that I occupied the easy chair.

"How can I help you?"

"We were wondering if we might search your house again?" he asked.

"This is getting repetitious, lieutenant. Do you have a search warrant?"

He shook his head. "But I can get one."

"You mean you can try to get one. If you had good cause to search my place, you'd have arrived with one." Being a published writer was clearly making me bold.

He gave a small smile. "You're right. A sympathetic judge might give it to me, but then again, he might not."

I waved my hand nonchalantly. "Search away. I give you my full permission."

"Thank you."

Cranston directed his sergeant to search the kitchen and the basement, while the uniformed officer headed up the stairs. Cranston sat with me for several moments in silence, leafing through his small note pad. I wondered if he'd learned this in some course where they taught that a prolonged period of quiet would break a suspect down.

Finally, he put the notebook away and spoke. "How have you been doing, Mrs. McAdams? It must be hard for you with your husband in jail."

"Not as hard as it is for him. Particularly since he didn't do it."

Cranston nodded. "A Mr. Ross Kennedy came to us making the same claim. Are you familiar with him?"

I nodded. "He was Amanda Beaumont's fiancé and a rather impressive man. He gave the eulogy at her funeral. I've heard that he's a psychologist and helping my husband with his case. I was surprised to hear that, given how much he must have loved the victim."

"He spoke to us and the district attorney. He came along with your husband's lawyer to give us a new view of things. They presented an interesting alternate theory of the crime. Even I found it somewhat compelling."

"But not compelling enough to get my husband out of jail."

"Not quite."

"What did he have to say?"

Although Kennedy had laid it all out for me during his visit to my house, I wasn't going to volunteer that I had spoken with him.

"You already know. Kennedy said that he had spoken to you."

"Ah, you mean his outlandish idea that I killed Amanda out of jealousy and framed my husband."

"We know that you visited the hotel once when your husband and Ms. Beaumont were working there. That indicates a jealous mind."

I smiled. "No. It indicates a good wife who had made her husband his favorite pie and wanted to bring him a piece."

"Seems a bit extreme to drive half an hour and disturb him in the middle of work to provide a piece of pie."

I shrugged. "It was a very good pie."

I was hardly paying attention to the lieutenant, being too busy listening to the men searching my house, waiting for one to shout "Hurrah!" and come running into the room with a piece of incriminating evidence that I had missed.

"There's also the matter of timing," Cranston went on.

"What about it?"

"Kennedy pointed out that you could have left shortly after you got back from your lunch and been at the Beaumont cottage at about the right time to murder Ms. Beaumont after your husband left. You'd still have been able to get home before your husband returned."

"Really. I'll have to think about that. However, after I came home from my luncheon appointment, I remained here until Jonathan returned at seven. Only after that did I go to see Amanda Beaumont."

"So you say."

"Yes, I do, and it's your job to prove differently."

"Kennedy's final point was that after killing Amanda with the fireplace poker, you brought it back here and placed it in your husband's car in order to make him appear guilty of the murder."

"Why would I try to incriminate my husband?"

"That's obvious. Because you thought he was having an affair with Amanda Beaumont."

I shook my head. "No, I didn't. Jonathan is a good-looking man and something of an incorrigible flirt, but I know that he's faithful to me."

"How can you be certain of that?"

"Because I know the man. He's a highly creative person, but like many creative people, he needs lots of emotional support. Jonathan frequently doubts himself and his ability, and he relies on me to provide him with balance so he can get through his daily life. Without me to keep him moored, he'd be completely adrift on a sea of self-doubt and anxiety. Deep down, Jonathan knows that, and he'd never risk our marriage. Certainly not by having an affair with an immature young woman, who, from what I've heard, was barely able to keep her own life together."

I could see that Cranston had been impressed by my last argument. We sat in silence for a while longer until his two men returned to the living room.

"Find anything?" Cranston asked. They both shook their heads. "Nothing at all?" Again, he got two negatives.

"What are you looking for?" Of course, I already knew, but I had to pretend like I didn't.

"Do you own a claw hammer?" Cranston asked.

"I believe that I've seen one around at various times," I said, hoping that he'd assume Jonathan, who didn't know a Phillips head from a flat-bladed screwdriver, did all our handyman work. It would be the sexist assumption to make.

"Can you recall the last time you saw it?"

"Probably the last time we hung a picture. That must be over a year ago."

"Where was the hammer usually kept?"

"All the tools we have are down in the cellar on the workbench, but I almost never go down there except to do laundry."

"It's odd that there's no hammer there."

"Maybe it got broken and was thrown away," I suggested.

"Hammers are made to hit things. They don't get broken very often," Cranston said.

"Look, if you're here because of the unfounded accusation that Ross Kennedy has been making, I'd suggest that you get back to him and ask if he has any proof to support the charges he's making."

The lieutenant stared at me. "I'm afraid we can't do that. Ross Kennedy was murdered last night in his hotel room. He was battered to death . . . with a hammer."

Chapter
Nineteen

I took a deep breath and let it out slowly the way I'd been taught to do by a yoga teacher back in the days when I had time to do yoga. I could feel my racing heart slow down and my mind calm. Things were bad, but not as bad as they would have been if I hadn't gone down into the cellar last night looking for a hammer.

"Where were you last night from five o'clock on?" Lieutenant Cranston asked.

"Right here," I said, except for when I was out back burying a bloody hammer, I didn't bother to add.

"What were you doing?"

"Eating, writing, and sleeping."

"What were you writing?"

"I'm helping Jonathan with the book he's working on." I didn't think that Jonathan would see it that way, but I wasn't going to go into details.

"The Duke Danforth book that he was writing with Ms. Beaumont?"

"Correct."

"So, you're writing it now?"

I nodded.

He paused to consider that but couldn't seem to find the question he wanted to ask.

"If I asked around the neighborhood, no one would have seen you drive away from the house after five last night?"

"Anyone who said they did would be mistaken."

Fortunately, it was after dark by now, but I wondered if they would be back tomorrow to search the property to look for the hammer. I hoped the hole I'd dug was as well concealed as I thought it was.

"Mr. Kennedy came back from New York City yesterday afternoon. That night someone came into his hotel room and murdered him."

"That's too bad."

"Have you spoken to him since he returned yesterday?

"No. The only time I spoke to him was when came here several days ago to try to intimidate me with his theory that I had murdered Amanda. I told him just what I told you, that I'm innocent. And that until he had some evidence to prove my guilt, I didn't want to see him again. I would also point out to you that Kennedy had as much motive, opportunity, and means as I did."

"It was rather foolish of him to come here alone, if he really thought you were a murderer."

"Maybe he didn't truly believe I was a violent killer."

"Or perhaps he was a bit too self-confident for his own good and that's what got him killed last night."

"Does this mean that Amanda's killer is still out on the loose, so you're going to let my husband out of jail?"

The lieutenant sighed. "We don't know that the same person killed Kennedy and Amanda Beaumont."

"You think there could be two killers out there bashing people's heads in?" I said, making my incredulity obvious.

"Your husband could have killed Amanda Beaumont, and someone else could have murdered Ross Kennedy." He looked at me as if he knew exactly who that someone else was. I could see that he was itching to put me in a cell right next to Jonathan, or worse yet, in Jonathan's cell after he was let free. Why not arrest me for both murders?

If I ended up arrested for Amanda's murder, I was sure Lynn would cancel my publishing contract in a heartbeat. She might even be desperate enough to give it back to Jonathan. I couldn't let that happen. I thought about Lynn's comment about Amanda and decided to try it on with Cranston.

"Amanda was the kind of girl who made enemies everywhere she went. I can't believe there aren't lots of possible suspects out there if you look hard enough."

"Oh, don't worry, Mrs. McAdams, we are going to keep searching." But by the way he was staring at me, I had a feeling that we didn't mean the same thing.

AFTER THE POLICE LEFT, I decided to have that glass of wine, but now it was less celebratory and more medicinal. I sat at the kitchen table, poured myself a large glass of red, and thought. My pleasant balloon of ecstasy over getting published had been punctured by the fear that I would lose it all as a result of being charged with the murder of Amanda, Ross Kennedy, or both. Someone clearly wanted to see me in a prison cell. I had been extraordinarily lucky to find the bloody hammer, but if I sat around passively waiting and doing nothing, eventually they'd find a way to incriminate me. I had to do something to discover who the real murderer was.

I decided to proceed on the working assumption that the same person had murdered both Amanda and Ross. Lieutenant Cranston might be right and there were two killers, but I still thought that the odds were against it. If Ross and Amanda hadn't known each other, the separate-killers scenario might have worked for me, but they were intimately connected. I had to believe that one person had a reason to kill them both.

As with all good hypotheses, the hard part was going to be coming up with a way to test it. How could I go about gathering evidence that would implicate someone else and keep me out of prison? I decided to begin with Amanda because she was the person most likely to have lots of enemies. Lynn had alluded to her unpopularity, but I needed specific names, and they had to be people who had been in the Great Barrington area recently. Kennedy probably had this information, but he had been too focused on accusing me to consider other people. And he was no longer available as a source of information. The only person I could think of who had spent a great deal of time with Amanda since she had moved to this area was Jonathan. Even if they hadn't been having an affair, there must have been some downtime from the writing when they'd discussed more personal things. Perhaps Amanda had mentioned someone in the area who had it in for her.

Tomorrow was Saturday, so I would have plenty of time to work on this. I'd begin by calling Jonathan's lawyer and seeing if I could set up a meeting with my husband. Even though the law office would be closed, the lawyer had given me his private cell phone number and told me to call him day or night if I'd had any concerns. And right now, I had lots of them.

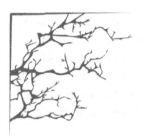

Chapter Twenty

The next morning, I waited impatiently until it was nine o'clock before calling Jonathan's lawyer. Since I was going to be asking a favor, I didn't want to annoy him upfront by bothering him early on a Saturday. To his credit, he answered right away and sounded alert, but when I told him why I was calling, he hesitated.

"I'd be happy to set up a visit for you with your husband," he said. "The problem is that your husband has specifically asked not to see you."

I was silent for a moment, too surprised to speak.

"Why not?" I finally asked.

"As you know, Ross Kennedy was assisting us for a brief time as part of the defense team, and he had a long conversation with Jonathan in which he presented his theory that you had murdered Amanda and framed your husband for the crime."

"I know, he came to my house and presented the same absurd theory to me."

"Yes, well . . . unfortunately, your husband was completely convinced by it, and he now believes that you also murdered Kennedy to prevent your guilt from coming to light. As a result, he is refusing to meet with you."

Poor Jonathan, the man was creative and clever, but when it came to reading people, he was sadly lacking. He could never see around his own ego long enough to understand what others were really like. I could easily imagine a charismatic man like Ross Kennedy convincing him that his wife of a decade, who had lovingly supported him through all sorts of adversity, was a brutal killer who wanted to see him in prison for her crimes. And once he seized on an idea, he would cling to it stubbornly in the face of any facts or emotional entreaties that I might present. I'd have to attempt to work around him.

"Well, perhaps you can help me," I said. "The most important matter I wanted to discuss with my husband was whether Amanda Beaumont had ever mentioned having any enemies who were staying in the area. Since I know that I did not kill Amanda or Ross, there must be someone else who had motive to do so, and I'm attempting to find out who that might be."

"Sarah, that kind of inquiry is probably best left to the police."

"Well, how much confidence do you have that the police, who already have a suspect in jail whom they believe they can convict, are going to investigate other avenues," I said. I tried to keep my tone reasonable, but I'm certain that some anger seeped out.

"Let me check my files online," he replied, a moment later. "I'll look through my notes on your husband's statement."

I sat for ten minutes singing softly to myself and hoping he found something that would prove helpful.

"It appears that your husband spent much more time sharing with Amanda than she did with him."

My heart sank. Jonathan always was better at talking than listening. I believe writers should spend more time asking questions than presenting opinions but that wasn't Jonathan's style. What an irony if he ended up in prison because he couldn't keep his mouth shut.

"There is one thing," the lawyer said. "Jonathan said that Amanda mentioned a woman she knew from down in the city who was spending the summer up here. Her name is Laura Hobart, and apparently, she was once the fiancé of Ross Kennedy. Amanda said something to Jonathan about hoping that she didn't run into her because the woman was crazy."

A crazy, jilted fiancé. What more could I hope for? I may have doubted Amanda's skill at determining whether someone was sane or not, but if Ross had dumped this woman for Amanda, she was very likely not too happy about it.

"Do you have a way of contacting her?"

"Yes. Amanda had her contact information on her phone. I thought that was a bit odd."

"Maybe she was following the adage to keep your friends close and your enemies closer. Do you know if the police have talked to her?"

"They did but in a somewhat cursory sort of way. She denied knowing anything about Amanda's death or having seen her during her stay up here."

"The cops were probably so focused on either Jonathan or me that they didn't check into her statement."

"That's possible."

"Thank you for your time and help."

"Ah, Sarah, if you are planning to speak with this woman, keep in mind that if your theory is correct, she might be guilty of a double homicide. You want to be very careful."

"Good advice. Thank you."

I decided that an unannounced visit on Laura Hobart would be best. If I called, she could refuse to see me, and even if she did agree, she'd have plenty of time to prepare her script. I wanted to see her first reaction when I showed up on her doorstep. I thought she might be willing to see me. After all, we were both women who had been done wrong by the predatory Amanda.

I left a note on the kitchen table stating where I was going. If I didn't return, at least the police would have some idea who the likely killer might be, and I'd have eventual revenge on my murderer. As part of a more short-range plan, I shoved a canister of pepper spray in the pocket of my jacket. I wasn't sure how skilled I'd be at using it because it had been a while ago since I read the directions. But how hard could it be? Point and shoot, just like a cheap camera.

I went out to my car and plugged my destination into the navigation system. Laura was living in a village right outside the boundaries of Great Barrington, so the location would have made it easy for her to dispatch Amanda. As I drove south, I considered my approach. Unfortunately, Laura wasn't likely to break down and confess just because I showed up on her doorstep looking suspicious. I'd have to gain her confidence by leaning hard on the betrayed sisterhood card. That might not work. Some women had no more use for sisters than they did for brothers. I'd just have to hope and improvise.

Twenty-five minutes later, I parked on the street in front of a small cottage, not unlike the one Jonathan and I occupied. I sat there for a moment, taking deep slow breaths. Once I felt halfway calm, I opened the door and headed up the walk to the house. I stood on the small porch and rang the bell. A few seconds later, a short, slightly plump but very pretty woman of around my age opened the door. She gave me a friendly smile. I immediately thought that she didn't look the least bit crazy. But then I remembered the things I'd read suggesting that sociopaths often looked and acted just like your next-door neighbor. They didn't come with warning labels on their foreheads.

"Can I help you?" she asked.

"Are you Laura Hobart?"

She nodded.

"I know that this might seem a bit strange, but I'm Sarah McAdams. My husband has been arrested for the murder of Amanda Beaumont, and I was wondering if I might talk with you."

Her smiled disappeared, but she held the door open and silently motioned for me to come inside. I checked quickly to see that neither of her hands held a hammer. We went into a living room that was not very different from mine, except for being somewhat better furnished. Now that I had book money coming in, I'd have to take care of that deficiency.

"Are you vacationing here for the summer?" I asked, thinking it would be best to start out slowly as I took a seat on the edge of the sofa, ready to get up and run if necessary.

"I'm a fashion designer and can pretty much work from anywhere, and I thought it would be nice to get out of the city for a while." She paused and looked down at her hands. "I also knew that Ross Kennedy was going to be up here on and off during the summer, and I thought that maybe we could get together some time."

"I heard from my husband's lawyer that the two of you were once close. I'm sorry for your loss."

"I just heard about his murder yesterday from some friends. It's very hard to believe that he's gone. He was so full of life."

"How did the two of you meet?"

"A few years ago, I was going through a hard time. I'd just broken up with my boyfriend, and the company I had been with for five years laid me off. I got really depressed. One of my friends recommended that I make an appointment with Ross, but he didn't have an opening on his patient list. But he offered to see me one time and make a referral to another doctor."

"Is that what happened?"

"Not exactly. After the first visit, Ross said that although he couldn't take on any new patients, perhaps we could get together informally and discuss my problems."

"So, were you like what . . . going out?"

"I guess you could call it that. We were dating, but much of the time, I'd be telling Ross about myself, and he'd be giving me advice. It usually turned out to be partly a date and partly therapy."

"How long did it go on?"

"For almost two years. And to be fair, I have to say I made a lot of progress because of him. I started to feel much better, and I had the confidence to get a new job. I owe much of that to Ross."

"And the two of you also got engaged?"

"That happened early on after we'd been going out for six months or so. I thought it was a little fast, but Ross really seemed to see us having a future together. I admit that having a handsome, successful man want to marry you is flattering and that's partly the reason why I said yes."

"Was it when he met Amanda that your relationship fell apart?"

Laura frowned. "I tend to blame Amanda for the whole thing because she came on the scene and made a big play for him. But if I'm being honest, our relationship had started to deteriorate before that. It happened when I began to get better. As our relationship became less therapeutic, Ross began to drift away. As I became stronger, he increasingly lost interest in me."

"Was it because he wanted you to be dependent on him?"

"Maybe. But I always believed that it had more to do with his self-image. He saw himself as a rescuer of women, and once the woman no longer needed rescuing, he moved on. Perhaps he didn't expect to be so successful with me, and when I quickly began to do well, there was nothing left in our relationship for him. I'm sure he came to regret that we'd ever gotten engaged."

"Did you have an opportunity to see him when he was up here?" I asked.

"I called him several times. He finally returned my call a few days before Amanda was murdered. We met for breakfast at the hotel where he was staying."

"So, he wasn't living with Amanda while he was up here?"

"No. He had his own room in the hotel. He used to call it keeping therapeutic distance. We never shared bedrooms either when we were together."

"How did your visit together that morning go?"

"Let's just say he made it very clear to me that anything between us was over and that he was completely devoted to Amanda."

"That must have hurt."

"I tried to explain to him that his attempt to cure every woman he met was self-destructive, because it meant that he would never have a happy, mature relationship. I know that intellectually he understood what I was saying, but he couldn't change."

"Amanda certainly needed him from what I've heard about her."

Laura's face hardened. "There's no doubt that Amanda had mental health issues, but even if she'd been well, she'd have been a bad person. She was hopelessly spoiled and manipulative, and I don't think anyone could cure her of that. If your husband did kill her, I'm sure he had good reason."

"Maybe so. But that won't help him in court. You know, shortly before Ross was killed, he came to me and accused me of murdering Amanda because she had tried to seduce my husband. I didn't, of course, but he seemed determined to prove it."

Laura frowned. "In his mind, Amanda being killed by another man would seem tawdry but being killed by the man's wife would make it seem as if she were the victim of a crazy woman. It was his last attempt to save her by rescuing her reputation."

"Ross sounds like a very complex man."

"Indeed, he was."

"You must have been very disappointed when he said that it was all over between you."

"Yes and no. I knew we'd never be together once I was cured, but I thought that now it was my job to cure him. To get him to leave Amanda before she destroyed him." She paused and tears filled her eyes. "But I couldn't do that. I couldn't return the favor."

I traveled back home thinking about how complicated people could be and that our rationality was only a thin veneer over the deeper needs and emotions that truly controlled us. And sometimes our obligations to other people carry on long after our reason tells us that the commitment is over.

Laura and I were flip sides of the same coin. Ross could only relate to woman that needed his help, and Jonathan could only relate to woman who could help him. When Laura could no longer provide him with a subject to serve, he dropped her. I knew that if I stopped supporting Jonathan, he would quickly replace me. I wondered which of us was worse off. In both cases, the men in our lives controlled things. Either you played by their rules, or it was over.

However, despite all these interesting insights, I wasn't sure it had gotten me any further down the road with my investigation. I just couldn't see Laura as Amanda's killer. She certainly hated the woman and thought she was a bad influence on Ross, but I think she knew that killing Amanda wouldn't bring Ross back to her. And as it turned out, even death didn't end Ross's infatuation with Amanda.

No, I decided that I would have to look elsewhere for a likely murder candidate. Unfortunately, I didn't know   where.

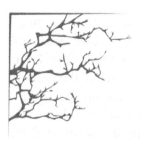

Chapter Twenty-One

I spent Saturday afternoon cleaning the house. I could hear my mother's voice telling me that having your husband accused of murder and yourself possibly the next on the list for incarceration was no excuse for keeping a dirty home. I'd neglected it long enough, and I must admit to feeling a sense of satisfaction when I collapsed on the sofa at the end of the day with everything set to rights.

The next day being Sunday, I went out and did some food shopping since the larder had gotten rather bare. In the back of my mind was the thought that the police might release Jonathan at any time. How long could they continue to believe that he had murdered Amanda now that Ross had been killed in a similar way? And Jonathan wouldn't be happy to arrive home and find that the fridge was empty. The rest of Sunday I devoted to preparing lesson plans, just in case Principal Clark decided to have a pop inspection of my recordkeeping.

The next day, as soon as I arrived at school, Clark motioned for me to come into his office. "I just wanted to let you know that as of the next school year, you will be teaching social studies at the middle school," he said with a smile of satisfaction. "Rhonda Pagoni had requested a transfer to high school history. She's senior to you, so we're required to give her preference."

"I've never heard of a high school teacher being bumped from her position for that reason."

"It's in the union contract. You can check."

"Maybe it's in the contract, but it's never been done in my time in the system."

He replied with a shrug.

I turned and walked out of the office, not giving him the satisfaction of seeing how angry I was. I'd taught social studies to seventh and eighth graders for three years when I first started, before I'd gotten my master's degree. It had been a tough slog. The discipline problems were more challenging on that level, and the material had to be presented in a very basic way. This was clearly an attempt by the administration to get me to quit. Well, that wasn't going to happen before the end of the school year, so I still had eight months to continue to be a thorn in their side.

When I returned home from school, I got into my house clothes and settled down behind Jonathan's computer, which I now thought of as mine. Lynn had sent me some suggestions for revisions yesterday, showing that she didn't spend her Sunday on domestic chores like I did. Heck, I thought, she probably had a maid, and since as far as I knew she was single, there was no man she had to cater to. That made it easier to have your life revolve around writing.

I had just settled in behind the computer and gotten my head into the story when the doorbell rang. Muttering to myself, I headed down the stairs, almost tripping on the raised area of carpet by the top step. I reminded myself that I'd have to purchase another hammer soon so I could fix it before I fell. As I approached the door, I set up a small prayer that it wouldn't be Lieutenant Cranston with more of his endless questions and accusations. It was getting to the point where I might not speak to him again without my lawyer present. Of course, I had yet to get a lawyer.

But it wasn't the lieutenant on the front porch. Instead, it was a woman in her late twenties. She was a couple of inches taller than I, lean and limber, with an aura of cross-country running and yogurt consumption about her. She was cute, with a perky ponytail that I was sure would bob up and down charmingly as she engaged in strenuous exercise. I figured she was collecting for something wholesome and community oriented.

"Hi," she said, sounding nervous. "Are you Mrs. McAdams?"

"That's right."

She stuck out a slender hand. "I'm Rachel Collins. I'm the chairperson of the English Department where your husband Jonathan works."

I took her hand. So, this was the old battleax that Jonathan was always complaining about. As I thought back, I realized that he had never really described her to me. It was his rendition of her various criticisms of his slack behavior that had led me to conjure up a woman in her sixties with a gray bun and stern, wrinkled face. I decided that Jonathan really could weave compelling fiction when he wanted to.

"Won't you come in," I said, standing back and directing her toward the living room, which was fortunately spotless for once. I didn't want things to look bad for Jonathan's boss.

"I suppose you might be wondering why I'm here," she said, when we were both seated.

I gave her a polite smile. I wasn't going to help her out.

"Those of us in the English Department have, of course, been aware from the newspaper stories that Jonathan is currently having difficulties." She stopped, then rushed on. "Let me first reassure you and your husband that his position is being held for him and will be available once this situation is resolved."

Since Jonathan might easily be sentenced to twenty years, I doubted that hers was an ironclad guarantee. But I decided not to debate the small points.

"Thank you. I'm sure that Jonathan will find some comfort in hearing that."

She nodded. "And you should know that none of us has . . . that I have no doubt as to his innocence."

I nodded. I was glad she'd limited the opinion to herself. Writers should be accurate, and I was reasonably certain that many of Jonathan's colleagues probably thought he was as guilty as sin. And a large fraction of those doubtlessly hoped he would be convicted. Jonathan tended to have that effect on people, especially men.

"You seem to have a high opinion of my husband," I said.

She blushed becomingly. "He's a very creative man. Most of us in English just talk about works of literature, but he creates them. You know what they say, 'Those that can't do, teach.'"

"Yes. I'm a teacher myself."

Now embarrassment made her blush. She paused, not sure how to go on. I had mercy on her.

"But creative people can sometimes be challenging in their own way," I said.

"Oh, I'm sure," she said, relieved to be able to agree with me.

"And from what Jonathan has told me, there have been times when you've had to replace the carrot with the stick."

She grinned. "Well, you know Jonathan, he sometimes can be a bit vague about his responsibilities. I can understand why he focuses on his writing more than teaching. But sometimes it's necessary for me to rein him in. I have a duty to the students who are paying for the course and the school itself."

"I completely understand. Even the most creative person needs to be brought down to earth on occasion."

"On the other hand, it is also my job to nurture . . . all members of my department. As the department chair, I'm required to encourage them so each can develop to his or her fullest potential."

I smiled and wondered exactly what form her nurturing of Jonathan had taken.

"But, of course, you know all this already. I'm sure that Jonathan would not have accomplished all he has without your love and support."

Damn right on that one, lady, I thought.

"We seem to work well together as a team," I replied, keeping my expression neutral.

"Although, I'm sure that working side-by-side with a creative can have its ups and downs. You must see it as a privilege to be the midwife to his efforts."

"Of course," I said, wondering what field of literature she specialized in, maybe it was purple prose.

Suddenly, her face became somber, and I thought she was going to cry.

"I was also wondering if you could tell me any more about Jonathan's legal situation. From what I've read in the newspapers, it sounds rather dire. And I've . . . we've . . . been very concerned about what the future holds for him."

"It's a bit up in the air for the moment."

"But surely the death of that murdered woman's fiancé while Jonathan was in jail must show that he's innocent."

I nodded. "You would think so, but the police are like a dog with a bone. They are very reluctant to release him without another suspect to arrest. The evidence against Jonathan is quite substantial though far from conclusive. But I'm afraid the police would need someone who looked even guiltier before they let him go."

"But are they even looking for anyone else?" she asked plaintively.

"Not as actively as one might hope. But I'm confident that further information will eventually become available that will exonerate him."

"I sincerely hope so."

I stood up. "Thank you for dropping by. I'll let Jonathan know about your visit. It will certainly help keep his spirits up in this difficult time."

She smiled with quivering lips. I opened my arms to indicate a sisterly hug, and she lurched across the room toward me. I held her as she sobbed softly on my shoulder. She clearly had girlish dreams of Jonathan, or, more accurately, what he represented. Such dreams could be very intoxicating. I knew. I'd once had them myself. But like most intoxicating things, they could take away your life before you knew it. I felt sorry for her, but also knew that there was no way I could cure her. But hopefully, there would come a time when she would realize the truth for herself.

While I held her in my arms, I gave her a tight squeeze. She was muscular and strong. I could easily imagine her wielding a fireplace poker or a hammer with sufficient force to kill. She had a soft, mothering personality, but I imagined there was fierceness underneath it all that would come out in defense of her beloved. I could easily see her bashing in Amanda's head, but what motive would she have had for killing Ross? Once again, my investigation was stymied.

"Will you stay in touch with me, so I know how Jonathan is doing?" she asked, as I walked her to the door.

"Of course," I said soothingly.

"Do you think it would be possible for me to see him?"

"I'll check with his lawyer, and he'll be in touch."

With a grateful smile and a final hand clasp she left, heading down the walk with an athletic stride. I would never arrange for her to visit Jonathan, not because I was jealous, but because I couldn't do that to her. I might not be able to end her adolescent addiction, but I wasn't going to be an enabler.

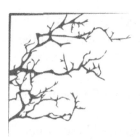

Chapter Twenty-Two

The next two weeks went by in a flash. Lynn negotiated a contract for me with Harrison Cole's publisher for the book I had just completed and for two more in the future. She was also correct that the advance on the current book was worth about two years of my teaching salary. With the money rolling in, I decided that I'd have to get an accountant soon to determine my tax liability. Shortly after the contract was signed, I had a pleasant phone conversation with Cole's longtime editor. She wanted a few changes made but was generally delighted with the manuscript that I had sent her, commenting that she'd rarely seen such a well-polished submission. Along with those good words, however, came the warning that I should immediately begin thinking about the next Duke Danforth thriller. Wash, rinse, and repeat was the order of the day.

Jonathan was still refusing to have me visit. I can't say I was very disappointed. I wasn't about to waste a lot of time defending myself against Ross Kennedy's baseless accusations. If Jonathan chose not to believe me, so much the worse for him. Not seeing him also allowed me to avoid discussing my newfound career as a writer. I was certain that would anger him as much as being in jail. I wanted him out of jail and would work hard to see it happen, but I didn't particularly want to spend time with him.

Lieutenant Cranston had also made himself scarce for the past two weeks, so I had no updates on whether the police were pursuing any new avenues or were simply content to hope they could win a conviction against Jonathan. I suspected it was the latter, which made me feel more and more responsible for discovering the truth. Unfortunately, I was struggling to come up with any new avenues to pursue myself. Both Laura Hobart and Rachel Collins had motive and opportunity for the murder of Amanda, but I couldn't see any reason for either of them to kill Ross Kennedy. Also, neither one of them seemed coldhearted or vicious enough to be going around bashing people on the head. Once again, however, I warned myself that appearances can be deceiving. What I needed was more evidence that pointed to one or the other of them, but it wasn't until I sat at my kitchen table on Saturday after lunch that a new avenue opened for me.

I'd been sitting there musing on the last words Ross Kennedy had said to me about going door-to-door through my neighborhood trying to find someone who saw me drive away during the time frame of Amanda's murder. Even though he'd been attempting to threaten me, I knew that I had been home, so he wouldn't have discovered anything. But that got me thinking that maybe canvassing a neighborhood might be a good idea. From my one visit on the night of the murder, I remembered that there had been a house directly across the street from Harrison Cole's cottage. I wondered if someone living there might have seen something of which the police were not aware. Almost a month had passed since Amanda's murder, a witness might come to remember something new long after the event that he or she had failed to report to the police. It was certainly worth a shot.

I dressed up in one of my teaching outfits so I'd look passably professional and headed out for the Cole cottage. It was a beautiful fall afternoon, and although most of the trees had lost their colorful leaves by now, there was something refreshing about the late fall with its memories of the summer and anticipation of the strenuous winter to come. Soon, Thanksgiving would arrive. I wondered if Jonathan would be celebrating it in jail. I imagined that prison turkey with all the fixings wouldn't be anything to write home about.

When I pulled up on the street in front of the Cole cottage, I discovered that my memory hadn't mislead me. There was a house directly across from it, quite near to the street, and with a fine view of the driveway leading up to Cole's front door. I parked along the curb and walked down a short drive to the house. I rang the bell and waited. Nothing happened, so I rang the bell again. I was about to give up and make plans to return tomorrow when the door opened, and two eyes peered out at me from about waist level.

"Hello," I said brightly. "I'm a friend of the Cole family, and I was wondering if you could answer a few questions for me."

"Are you from the newspapers?" a quavering voice asked.

"Nope. Just a friend of the family."

That seemed to do the trick. The door opened to reveal a very short woman leaning on two canes.

"I'm sorry that it took me so long to answer the door. I don't have my caregiver on weekends, and I'm slow getting around because of arthritis. Would you like to come in?"

I followed her inside and waited while she carefully locked the front door.

"Can't be too careful," she said, and I nodded my agreement.

We went to the right, into a dark, cavernous living room that had been furnished in an earlier time. I was pleased to see that there was a large bay window looking out directly on the driveway up to the Cole cottage. I was even more pleased to see that what appeared to be a well-used easy chair was in front of the window with a pair of binoculars on the end table next it.

"I'm Muriel Goldsmith," the woman said. "Forgive me for not extending my hand, but I need to hold both canes to keep from tipping over."

"I'm Sarah Lane," I lied. I was afraid that, if she was sharp enough, the name McAdams might ring a bell with her from all the news coverage Jonathan had received, and she'd toss me out. I was surprised how natural it felt to use my family name.

She pointed to an upholstered chair across from the easy chair by the window. I sat. She slowly settled into her chair and breathed a sigh of relief.

"I'm afraid that I use up most of my energy these days just standing and walking around the house. My caregiver usually brings me what I need, which is very nice. Although I suppose doing for myself is important if I don't want my condition to worsen. Life always seems to consist of difficult choices."

I nodded. "I notice that you have quite a view from there," I said, indicating the window.

"Oh, yes. I love to watch the season's change. Of course, as you get older the passage of time becomes a bit bittersweet. But it does give me a sense of being a part of things. It also gives me a chance to watch the world go by."

"And you have binoculars as well. Do you like to watch the birds?"

"My late husband, Gordon, was more for that than I am." She paused as if uncertain how much to say. "If I'm being honest, I have to admit that I use the binoculars mostly to keep an eye on the Harrison Cole house."

"Were you friends with Harrison Cole?" I asked.

"Oh, yes. He was a lovely man. Gordon and I used to have dinner occasionally with Harrison and Grace. After our spouses died, Harrison would come over once a week or so, and we'd have tea together in the afternoon. He'd talk about what he was writing and the people he knew in publishing. It was fascinating to get an inside glimpse into such an interesting industry. He was also a great reader, as am I, and we'd often exchange suggestions about books to read and discuss them together afterward. It was a great loss to me when he passed away," she said wistfully.

"Did you watch the house in order to look out for his safety?"

She nodded. "We had an arrangement. When he was going to be away, he'd tell me in advance, and I was to call the police if I spotted anything unusual. When he was home, he opened the drapes in his study, which I can see from here with the binoculars. If they weren't opened by nine o'clock, I was to call the police. I was the one who called the police when he had his accident. On weekends when my caregiver is away, I'd open this curtain right here by nine. If he didn't see it, he'd come right over to check on me. Occasionally, I'd forget." She smiled mischievously, "Mostly it was on purpose because then Harrison would stay for breakfast"

"Did you get to know his granddaughter, Amanda?"

"Very little. Harrison brought her over once to meet me, but I could tell she was the kind of young person who had little interest in old people. So few young people seem to realize that someday they'll be like us."

"Did you see her more after she moved in?"

Muriel shook her head. "Not to speak to. I frequently saw her pull into the driveway and walk to the front door, but she never came over to see me. But a young woman living alone like that, I worried about her, and felt I should look after her out of respect for Harrison's memory."

"That was very thoughtful of you. Did the police question you concerning what you saw the night of Amanda's murder?"

She nodded. "A young man wearing a policeman's uniform who hardly looked old enough to be out of school came over and asked me a few questions. I told him that I saw a car arrive at about twelve-thirty in the afternoon, and a man whom I'd seen there several times before went into the house."

I figured that must be Jonathan.

"The same man left in quite a hurry around five o'clock."

"Did you see anyone else arrive?"

"A car pulled into the driveway around eight, but I couldn't see who got out of the car because the porch lights weren't on."

That was when I had arrived. Muriel's recollections were accurate, but so far they hadn't provided me with anything new.

"After that, the police came and all sorts of other vehicles arrived."

"Did you see any other cars pull into the driveway that night before the police arrived?"

She shook her head. "That's what the young officer asked, and I told them I hadn't. But since then, I've begun to think about that question more broadly."

"What do you mean?"

"Well, I didn't see another car pull into the driveway, but there was a car that parked on the street a little way up."

"What time was this?"

"I'd say around five forty-five or so. After the man left and before the second car arrived."

"Did you see someone get out of the car?" I could feel my heart rate increase. I hoped I was on to something.

"Yes. There is a streetlight about twenty feet from the bottom of the Cole's driveway. I saw a person walk under it and go up the driveway."

"Can you describe what the person looked like?"

"That's hard to do, my dear, because whoever it was wore a jacket with the hood up, so I couldn't make out much of their appearance."

"Do you think it was a man or a woman?"

"From this distance there's no way I can be sure. And today lots of boys and girls look pretty much the same to me."

I smiled to myself. "How about the person's height? Tall or short?"

Muriel smiled. "I'm afraid that everyone seems tall to me. And I was seeing them from across the street."

I thought about whether there was some way I could get a better description.

"What if I went across the street? Could you get a sense of whether the person was shorter or taller than me?"

"That might help. Especially if you stood next to the tree near the bottom of the driveway because I remember the person paused there for a moment."

I got up and left the house. I went across the street to the tree Muriel had indicated. I stood next to it attempting to appear stealthy. After striking a couple of different poses, feeling like I was doing a photo-op for *Murderer Weekly*, I went back to the house. Muriel was standing up and met me at the door.

"What do you think? Was the person taller or shorter than I am?"

"It's very hard to tell, I'm afraid. But I believe the person was of about the same height as you."

"Was the person thinner or heavier than I am?"

"Perhaps a bit fuller in the body than you."

I paused to think. This wasn't proving very helpful. Laura Hobart was heavier than me, but also considerably shorter, and Rachel Collins was both thinner than me and taller. Neither of them seemed to fit the description Muriel had given.

"I really should be able to do better than this," Muriel said. "After all, I've seen the person twice."

I quickly turned to her. "Excuse me."

"Well, the first time I saw that person was on the night that Harrison Cole had his accident."

"Are you sure it was the same person?"

"The person was dressed the same, parked in the same place, and certainly appeared to be the same individual as far as I can tell."

"Did you tell the police?"

"They never came around after Harrison fell. After all, why would they question the neighbors about an accident?"

So, the mysterious visitor who had visited the cottage twice when people died had never been mentioned to the police. That was an interesting piece of information that only I possessed.

"Thank you for your assistance, Muriel," I said, touching her arm.

"Sorry I couldn't be of more help, but I hope what I told you was somewhat useful."

"I think it may be, once I've had time to fully consider it."

Muriel cocked her head inquisitively. "Do you like to read?"

I was about to say that I read occasionally, but I realized that now that I'd become an author, I'd also have to become a regular reader.

"Yes. Actually, I do."

"Wonderful." Muriel slowly made her way over to a table near the front door. A pad and pen were there. Leaning against the table, she released one of her canes and used her free hand to write on the pad.

"Here's my phone number," she said, indicating the right hand that now held both the cane and the piece of paper.

I took the paper from her hand.

"Give me a call, and perhaps we can arrange to get together sometime for tea and discuss a book we've both read. She paused. "Of course, only if you'd like to do that."

I smiled. "I'd like to do that. I'd like to do that very much, Muriel."

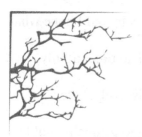

Chapter Twenty-Three

I was sitting at the kitchen table over a cup of tea, having just finished my microwave dinner. I was still mulling over what I had learned from Muriel. The fact that possibly the same person had been at the Cole cottage the night Harrison died and the night his granddaughter had been murdered put a whole new focus on my investigation. Before, I'd been concentrating solely on people who would have wanted Ross and Amanda dead. But now the further question raised was, who wanted Harrison Cole dead? Had his death been a murder rather than an accident?

An ugly thought came into my mind. Who had gained the most from Harrison Cole's accident. It wasn't Amanda, since he had apparently left her little or nothing in his will. The only person I could think of who stood to gain substantially was Jonathan, being the next in line to write the Duke Danforth novels. When he first mentioned it to me, he had pretended that he hadn't taken Cole's offer seriously because he was angry over not getting credit for the novel he had helped him write. But what if Jonathan had been telling me a modified version of the truth. He'd certainly done that before when he had failed to inform me that he knew Cole quite well. If Jonathan had believed Cole was really going to make him the heir to Danforth novels, I might see him wanting to hurry the old man along to his final reward, especially since Harrison seemed to be showing a renewed vitality. Jonathan would find the idea of waiting another ten years to claim his literary inheritance to be unacceptable.

And then, just when Jonathan thought everything was set, Amanda came along and once again tried to snatch success from his waiting hands. That would certainly give hm a motive for killing her. I considered the time frame and what Muriel had observed. She had seen Jonathan leave at five o'clock, just as he said. But what if he returned at quarter to six, having thought things over and decided that Amanda had to be eliminated. He often carried a dark hoodie in the back of his car in case of rain, so Jonathan could easily have slipped it on, murdered Amanda, and driven home by seven.

It was a compelling scenario, but there were two things about it that I didn't like. First, I had been married to Jonathan for ten years. Now granted, he could be moody when things didn't go his way and huffy when his opinion was questioned. But I had never known him to be physically violent. He tried to get his way by sulking, not by using his fists. Now I know that you often read stories about wives who remained oblivious to the fact that their husbands were serial killers, but I'd never fully believed that. Deep down, I thought there had been plenty of indications that the women, for their own reasons or needs, had chosen to ignore. I thought I had a clear-eyed picture of Jonathan, warts and all, and he wouldn't go around killing people, even to secure his literary reputation.

The second problem with the scenario is that it didn't explain why Ross Kennedy had been killed. Jonathan had been in jail at the time of that murder, so he couldn't be responsible. And, in fact, Kennedy was involved in helping him get out of jail at the time he was murdered. Jonathan had every reason to want him to stay alive. So, someone else must have wanted Ross dead for some other reason.

I knew that if I called Lieutenant Cranston and presented him with my new information, he'd fix me with his level stare and say that there were probably two killers: Jonathan and an unknown person who didn't like Ross Kennedy. That wouldn't help get Jonathan out of jail, which was my primary goal. I had to come up with a suspect who had wanted all three people dead, and right now, Ross Kennedy's murder was the hardest to explain.

I took several deep breaths and tried to relax my mind. Slowly, I focused on the last time I had seen Kennedy alive. He had just presented his preposterous theory that I had murdered Amanda. What had he said next? It finally came to me that was when he'd stated his intention to survey my neighborhood for someone who had seen me leave earlier than I had said on the night Amanda was killed. But he had never gotten around to doing that because he had to go back to New York to meet with his patients. Who, other than myself, would have known his plans and felt threatened by them? I felt the need to talk this over with someone else, someone who would have an unbiased perspective.

The front doorbell rang, disturbing my train of thought. It was dark out, so I put the chain on the front door before opening it. Maggie stood on the porch.

"Hey, Sarah, I just wondered if you had a minute."

I opened the door. "Sure. C'mon inside and have a seat. I've finished eating."

Wearing one of her mismatched sweatsuits, Maggie settled onto the sofa.

"The munchkins are staying at friends' houses tonight, so I thought I'd pop over for a few minutes. You know, my oldest is about to start in middle school, and I just wanted your advice about something."

"I might have her in class," I said, my chest clenching at the prospect of being back on that level. "The school system is demoting me back to eighth grade level."

"Why?"

"Because of Jonathan being in jail. Having me on the faculty is an embarrassment to them, and they're trying their best to get me to quit."

Maggie shook her head. "This whole business with Jonathan has been nothing but a headache for everyone. How is he holding up?"

"Not too well. I really don't think he can survive prison life. I've been doing my best to try to find the real killer, but so far, I've had no luck. Every lead I've followed has come to a dead end. And now

179

Jonathan has been convinced by the late Ross Kennedy that I killed Amanda and tried to frame him."

Maggie shook her head. "I know Jonathan is wrong about you being the killer, but maybe the only way you can save him is by confessing that you did it."

I stared at her, waiting for the punchline. Maggie always did have an offbeat sense of humor. But none came.

I gave her a nervous smile. "You can't be serious. Why would I confess to something I didn't do?"

"To save Jonathan. After all, he's a creative genius. What are we by comparison?"

I almost told her that I had taken over the Duke Danforth thrillers, so I was pretty creative as well. In fact, I had proven to be the truly creative one. But I decided that would sound too much like bragging or hitting Jonathan when he was down.

Maggie reached in the pocket of her sweatshirt and a gun appeared in her right hand. I had to look twice before I believed my eyes.

"In a few minutes, Sarah, we're going to go upstairs, and you're going to use Jonathan's computer to write your confession. You'll take responsibility for killing Amanda out of jealousy, and then murdering Ross when he began to suspect you. After that, sadly, you are going to use this gun to commit suicide."

"Where would I have gotten a gun?" I asked, desperately seeking a flaw in her plan.

"When the police check, they'll find that this gun is registered to Jonathan. He bought it for me two months ago when I told him I didn't feel safe. The police will have no doubt how you got the gun because it was here in the house all along."

"Why would Jonathan buy you a gun?"

"Because we've been lovers for the last six months, and he cares for me."

I sank back into the sofa. "You and Jonathan?"

She smiled. "Surprising, isn't it. I may not appear to be much, but I have hidden resources. At first, Jonathan and I would just get together to talk about things. He'd tell me about writing and his ambitions, and I'd talk about wanting something more than just being a mother and a computer geek. And it just grew from there. You know, Jonathan really felt that you weren't supporting him enough anymore. That you had become more interested in your career as a teacher than in helping him to become the great writer he had the potential to be. We decided that it was time for me to take over."

My mind whirled. Another woman had been bamboozled by Jonathan, but this time it was someone who was truly crazy. I needed to do something, but the hand that held the gun stayed steady and pointed at the center of my chest.

"I'm sure that Jonathan didn't decide to leave me," I said.

Her lips tightened. "He would have in time. In a few more months, he'd have found the strength to leave you and be with me."

"He'd never do that."

"Then I would have solved the problem another way," she said, thrusting the gun in my direction.

"Killing someone is serious, Maggie. If you put that gun away and leave now, we'll never talk about this event again."

Maggie laughed. "I know how serious killing people can be. You wouldn't be my first. That was my husband. My dear, chronically unfaithful husband had such a surprised look on his face when I hit him on the head with that iron frying pan. That look alone was worth the effort of hitting him. He's buried out in the back near the oak tree bordering the pastureland."

"Did you also kill Amanda?"

"Of course. She's the only woman I've killed up until today. And I have to say it was a pleasure. When Jonathan called me on his phone right after his fight with her, I told him to come home, and I'd take care of it. If only he'd followed directions and come straight back here, he'd never have been a suspect. But you know how Jonathan is. He has a fantastic imagination but can be a little weak in common sense. He decided to drive around for a couple of hours and make himself look guilty. Then he let you go out there and muddy things up even more." She gave a gentle sigh as if forgiving all of Jonathan's foibles.

"And I bet you murdered Harrison Cole as well?"

Maggie's eyes got mean and they fixed on me. "How do you know that?"

"Unlike Jonathan, I can put two and two together."

She nodded. "He had promised to share credit for the book Jonathan almost single-handedly wrote, but then he reneged and said that instead he'd put Jonathan in his will as his successor. I went out to see him, pretending to be Jonathan's agent. I got Cole to show me his will, which guaranteed that Jonathan got first shot at being his literary successor. That sealed his fate. I pretended that I was fascinated with his cottage, and he was happy to show me around. Unfortunately, at the top of the stairs he tripped and had a little accident. After all, Cole couldn't really have expected Jonathan to wait around for years to start his career."

"And why did you kill Ross?"

"Oh, that's really your fault. You told me he was going to canvas the neighborhood to see if you'd left the house earlier than you said. I just couldn't be sure that someone might not say that they saw me leave at just the right time. Ross might have latched onto that and done some digging that would have created a problem for me. So, I called him at his office in New York and set up a meeting for his first evening back up here. He told me his room number, so I didn't have to go to the reservations desk like you did. Then I went to see him with the hammer I'd borrowed from your basement. He was angry when I first hit him. I think he took it as an insult. By the second blow he was afraid, but by then it was too late. Another man who had underestimated me. By the way, whatever happened to that hammer I put back in your house. Why didn't the police find it?"

I shrugged.

She smiled. "That's okay, Sarah, keep your secrets. Pretty soon they'll be safe with you forever. Now I think it's time we got on with it, don't you?"

"Jonathan will never marry you, you know," I said angrily.

"Of course he will. Unlike you, I've raised two children and know how to be self-sacrificing and nurturing. I know how to put myself second." She stood up. "On your feet, we have some work to do."

My knees shook as I made my way out of the living room with Maggie following close behind. I thought about running. Shooting me in the back would spoil her suicide story, but I had a bad feeling that she was capable of improvising an equally convincing alternative and wouldn't hesitate to shoot. We went upstairs, and I sat in front of the computer where I had recently experienced such joy. It seemed bitterly ironic that this was where I would meet my end. Maggie stood over me to my left, her gun pointed directly at the side of my head.

I began to type my confession, basing it largely on Ross Kennedy's version of events. I made a few typos out of nervousness. Maggie wanted me to leave them because they showed my agitated state of mind, but I refused. I wasn't going out leaving behind a poorly edited paragraph. When I was done, I checked it over while Maggie read over my shoulder.

"Don't you think you should express more remorse for what you've done?" she asked.

My God, I thought, there's always a critic up to the last.

"I don't think very many serial killers express a lot of regrets for what they've done. Do you?" I asked.

Maggie chuckled. "I suppose you're right."

"You know the authorities aren't going to be fooled by this suicide scenario. They'll figure out it was staged."

"I'm not so sure of that. I'll wipe my prints off the gun and press your fingers on the handle and trigger. I'll drop the gun right where it would have fallen from your hand. It'll appear convincing, and I'm betting that the cops will be very happy to wrap up this whole crime wave with a handy confession from a frustrated woman. Let's face it, they aren't going to look very hard if it means taking on more work and bad publicity."

I figured she was likely right. I read over the paragraph in front of me once more and decided it was pretty good prose. I thought it appropriate that I go out with a piece of decent fiction. Much of my life so far had been based on fiction. The fiction that my husband loved me, that my colleagues at school respected me, and that my next-door neighbor could be counted on for good advice. Now I knew there was very little that I could count on other than my own determination.

"There's one thing I don't understand?" Maggie asked.

I turned to my left to look up at her. Hoping to prolong my life by a few minutes.

"Why were the police so convinced that Jonathan murdered Amanda? Wasn't the evidence purely circumstantial?"

"It was probably because they found the fireplace poker under the floor of his trunk."

Maggie got a puzzled look. "I left it on the floor next to her head. How did it . . .?"

I could see her mind begin to work and her attention drifted from me for a second and the gun lowered slightly. I spun around to my left in the desk chair and grabbed her right hand with my left. The gun went off, deafening me but aimed toward the back wall. At the same time my right hand scooped Jonathan's commando knife off the desk, and I plunged it into Maggie's upper leg.

I struggled to my feet as she fell backward into the bookcase behind her. Her face was a mask of shock and pain, but she was still struggling to bring the gun around toward me. I turned and ran. Another shot was fired as I flew through the door and splinters of the doorframe stung the side of my face. Before I reached the stairs, I could hear her coming after me, bumping into things but making surprisingly swift progress.

I raced down the stairs, my feet skipping over some of the steps. When I reached the bottom, I turned to risk a glance behind me. Maggie had just reached the top step. She pointed the gun down at me and took a step forward to get a better shot. The foot she was dragging snagged on the raised rug at the top of the stairs. Unable to catch her balance due to her wounded leg, she fell head over heels down the wooden staircase.

She came to rest at the bottom of the steps, almost at my feet. She looked up at me and by the light in her eyes I could see that she knew. Then her eyes went dim, and she didn't know anything anymore.

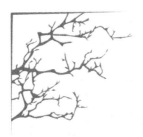

Chapter Twenty-Four

I was sitting in the easy chair in my living room.
Lieutenant Cranston was on the sofa with his rumpled
raincoat spread out around him like a shabby dress.
The medical examiner and the forensics people had
already been and gone, taking away Maggie's body.
I'd recited my version of events to a uniformed
officer and just completed doing the same thing for
Cranston. With all this repetition, I felt like an actor
having the misfortune of being saddled with a very
demanding director. It was getting on for eleven, and
I'd had a hard night by almost anyone's definition,
and my patience was wearing thin.

"I'll admit that the story you're telling us does
account for at least most of the facts," Cranston
admitted. "Let's go over it once again point by point."

"Can't this wait until tomorrow?" I asked.

"We'd like to get started confirming the facts
tomorrow, so it would help if we had all the
information clearly written down tonight."

I nodded.

"Now, you claim that Maggie Boyd told you that she murdered her husband about five years ago, is that right?"

"She said that she hit him on the head with a cast iron frying pan." I figured that the more detail I gave, the more plausible my story would seem.

"And she said that she buried him out back on her property?"

"By the oak tree near the end of her land."

And that all happened before you moved here?"

"Two years before."

"So, you never knew her husband. But you've heard that her husband cheated on her?"

"No, I never knew him. The rumor was that he was unfaithful and left her for another woman."

Cranston checked off something in his notebook.

"Then she told you that she had killed Harrison Cole because he backed out of an arrangement with your husband."

"Cole had promised my husband equal credit for helping him write his last book but changed his mind at the last minute."

"When was this agreement made."

"According to my husband, they came to the agreement six months ago. I only found out about it last month."

"Your husband didn't inform you at the time."

"I had no idea he had even written the book until a few weeks ago."

"But Cole promised your husband that he'd put it in his will that your husband could have an opportunity to take over writing the Duke Danforth novels at his death."

"That's what Jonathan told me."

"And Maggie Boyd murdered Harrison Cole so your husband could take over sooner?"

"Yes."

"Was your husband aware that she did this?"

"Not to my knowledge."

Cranston made another note to himself.

"And Boyd told you that she killed Amanda Beaumont because she was threatening to have your husband removed from the Cole writing project?"

"Yes. That's what she indicated."

"And you said that the woman across the street, a Muriel Goldsmith, says that she saw someone walk from a parked car to the door that night. Someone she couldn't identify."

"And she thought it was the same person who went to the house the night Harrison Cole had his so-called accident."

"Right. And Maggie Boyd also admitted to killing Ross Kennedy because she was afraid that if he canvassed the neighborhood, he would discover that she had driven away during the time frame of Beaumont's murder."

"I think she was getting a shade paranoid by then. But she was afraid that if Ross found out she had gone somewhere at the time of the killing, he might have dug into it and discovered some incriminating evidence."

The lieutenant nodded. "You also mentioned that Boyd said she had taken the fireplace poker she'd used to kill Amanda and placed it in your husband's car. Why would she attempt to incriminate your husband? To me that just doesn't make sense."

"All I can figure is that she did it at night. Both of our cars were out in the driveway and the nearest streetlamp is far away. The cars are the same make and model. My car is dark blue and Jonathan's is black. I think she just mixed up the colors. She wanted to incriminate me but put the poker in the wrong trunk."

"Huh. Well, I guess that is one explanation," Cranston said. He wrote something in his pad and circled it.

"Does this mean that Jonathan will be released from jail? After all, you have another person who's admitted to the murder he's accused of committing."

Cranston sighed and put the pad in his coat pocket. "You see, the problem is, you're the only one who heard her admit to all this. And you're not exactly an unbiased witness."

"Can't you find evidence to prove what she said?"

"We have no evidence that Harrison Cole was even murdered, and there is no proof that Boyd killed Amanda Beaumont or Ross Kennedy."

"Well, I can tell you, she certainly planned to murder me."

"Unfortunately, there's no proof of that either. The gun belonged to your husband, so for all we know, you were the one who threatened her with it."

"Ask my husband. He bought it for her."

"Of course, he'll say that."

I couldn't believe that the confession of a serial killer wasn't good enough to get Jonathan out of jail. The whole thing seemed crazy.

"Then go dig up her husband," I said. "He's out there near the oak tree somewhere. Don't you have equipment with sonar or x-rays or something that can see beneath the ground, or what about using cadaver dogs."

Cranston looked thoughtful. "I'll look into that in the morning."

"If you do find his body, wouldn't that be enough evidence to prove that Maggie's entire story is true?"

The detective paused before speaking. "It might be."

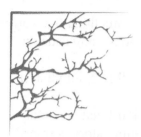

Chapter Twenty-Five

T he next afternoon, a police team showed up at Maggie's house. I heard that her children had been taken from the friends where they were staying the night before and had been placed with a relative. This was going to be the hardest for them. Maggie's obsession with Jonathan had been so strong that she failed to calculate the consequences for her children if she were discovered. But probably people like Maggie are so confident in their abilities to fool others that they never consider the possibility of being caught. She dressed and acted so that people, men in particular, would underestimate her. It had served her well, until she had underestimated me and my desire to continue writing. Maggie had never expected that I would fight to the last.

I guess finding a body that's been in the ground for five years is a challenging job because it wasn't until the next afternoon that I heard some loud shouting that indicated success. More people arrived on the scene, and a few hours later I saw a body bag being carried across the field. Now I could only hope

that what they had found would be the key to getting
Jonathan released from prison.

THE NEXT DAY, RIGHT after I had gotten home
from school and changed my clothes, the front
doorbell rang. Lieutenant Cranston stood on my
doorstep.

"May I speak with you for a few moments, Mrs.
McAdams?" he asked.

I nodded, and we went into the living room.

"Although I'm sure your husband's attorney will
be informing you shortly, I wanted to let you know
myself that we have found the body of a man whom
we believe to be Ronald Boyd, Maggie's husband.
The preliminary findings are that he died of a
fractured skull."

"Does that mean my husband will be released
from jail?"

"In the light of these findings, the district attorney
will be dropping all charges against your husband in
the next couple of days."

"Wonderful!"

The lieutenant sat on the sofa looking
uncomfortable.

"Is there something bothering you Lieutenant
Cranston? Do you still have doubts about Maggie
Boyd's guilt?"

"No," he said and paused. "But I still have one
question that's been bothering me. It doesn't seem to
quite fit with the story Maggie told you?"

"Oh, what's that?"

"You said that she claimed that the fireplace poker ended up in your husband's car because she mixed up the colors of the two cars."

"She never said that exactly," I replied. "That was my explanation of how such a mistake could have been made."

Cranston rubbed his forehead. "You see, the one problem with that explanation is that when I came around last night after dark and walked down the street from the direction of the Boyd house to your driveway, it was pretty obvious to me, even in the dim light, which car was black and which was blue. I just can't understand how she could have made such a mistake."

"She'd just murdered a person that evening, so Maggie was probably under a lot of stress. Errors occur when we're under stress."

"That's true," he agreed. "But Maggie Boyd doesn't sound to me like a woman who was very familiar with stress. She always kept a cool head."

I shrugged. "Everyone has an off day. Other than that, I really can't explain how she made that mistake."

"Yeah. Neither can I, and it bothers me," he said, rubbing his head again.

I almost told him that his *Columbo* routine was getting a bit old, what with the raincoat and the forehead rubbing. But I had a feeling that maybe he had never seen *Columbo*, and this was Cranston just being himself.

"Do all your cases end with the loose ends all tied up in a pretty bow?" I asked.

194

He gave me the first genuine smile I'd ever gotten from him.

"Good point. You're right, they don't every time."

"And does it always bother you?"

"I'm afraid it does," he sighed. "But I guess that's my problem, not yours."

"There's nothing wrong with being a perfectionist."

He smiled. "Now that your husband is getting out, will he return to writing the Duke Danforth thrillers?"

"No. I'll be the one taking over that project."

His eyebrows went up in surprise. "I didn't know that you were a writer."

"Neither did I. I started out writing to help Jonathan while he was in jail, and I discovered my hidden muse."

"Won't he be disappointed not to be the one writing them?"

"Disappointment is part of life, lieutenant. You're left with unanswered questions and Jonathan without a book contract." I knew that sounded a bit blunt, but I was getting tired of all this verbal fencing.

Cranston got to his feet. "I'll look forward to reading the next Danforth novel. I'm sure it will be a good one. You strike me as a fine storyteller."

"I try, lieutenant. I try."

After I showed him out the door, I took a deep breath and let it out slowly. He was a little too good at this *Columbo* routine.

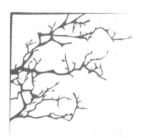

Chapter Twenty-Six

 As Cranston had predicted, the next day I got a call from Jonathan's lawyer telling me that all charges against him had been dropped. The official paperwork wouldn't be finalized for three more days, but then he would be released. I told him that I'd personally pick Jonathan up at the jail, and he promised to call in a couple of days to tell me the exact time to be there.

Three days put me on a rather tight schedule. I went online for names and then immediately called a local rental agent. She promised that there were a couple of furnished apartments available in the area I desired, and I arranged to see them with her tomorrow after school. Then I went down in the basement and pulled out the two old suitcases we'd used for our cultural excursions to New York City over the years. I dragged them up to my bedroom and filled them with the clothes from Jonathan's side of the closet and dresser. Since he usually dressed with a studied casualness for school in a button-down shirt and jeans—probably in order to demonstrate the creative artist's contempt for the business world with its suits and ties—it was easy to fit all his clothes in the two suitcases. One suitcase, of course, was officially mine, but I was more than willing to sacrifice it for the cause.

When I was done in the bedroom, I went back down to the basement and found two cardboard boxes left over from when we had moved into the house. I headed back up to the study. I opened the file cabinet and removed all the paper notes and manuscripts Jonathan had collected over the years and deposited them in the boxes. I had purchased a new laptop computer last week to do my writing on. It was a present to myself that I knew would come in useful. So, after carefully removing all my files from Jonathan's laptop, I tossed that in on top of the papers.

The boxes were heavy and carrying them down the stairs required some care. Fortunately, I had purchased a new hammer a few days ago and repaired the ripped carpeting at the top of the stairs. Although I didn't believe that Maggie's ghost was lurking about the house somewhere, ready to trip me up, I had no intention of tempting fate. As we're always warned, most accidents happen in the home.

When I'd finally gotten all of Jonathan's stuff loaded into the back of the car, I called the college where he worked and asked to speak to the chair of the English Department. Fortunately, Rachel Collins was available and quickly picked up the phone.

"Hello, Mrs. McAdams, how can I help you?" she asked, sounding genuinely glad to hear from me.

"Please call me Sarah. I just wanted to let you know that I've been informed by his lawyer that

Jonathan will be released and all charges against him dropped by the end of the week. I thought you should know in case it impacted your scheduling of courses."

"That's very considerate of you. Since we're already into November, I don't think it would be wise to have Jonathan come back right now. But I do have several writing courses open for the spring semester. Fortunately, I might be able to give him three courses rather than his usual two. That should help him make up for any income he's lost this semester."

"I'm sure he'll appreciate that," I said. I had a funny picture in my mind of Jonathan cursing from under a pile of student writing assignments. "I'll send you an email in the next couple of days with his new address in case you need it for contract purposes."

"Oh, you're moving."

"No, Jonathan is."

"I see," Rachel said. There was a prolonged silence.

"Jonathan and I are separating, and I'll be filing for divorce."

"I'm very sorry to hear that."

I didn't believe she was for a minute, but I thought that she should be. Jonathan on his own without a woman to support him was like a negative charge without a positive charge. He'd gravitate toward the first woman who smiled and seemed enthralled by his narrative about his own genius. In our first meeting, Rachel had seemed to me to be halfway to believing it already. Now that Jonathan was free floating, she was most likely doomed. I searched my mind for something to say that would warn her off. I could tell her that Jonathan had cheated on me, but she'd probably blame that on some deficiency in me that had forced Jonathan to seek solace elsewhere. I could list all of Jonathan's weaknesses and deficiencies, but she'd perceive that as my inability to appreciate his overwhelming strengths, which to her mind far outweighed his minor flaws. Only hard-won experience, I feared, would help her see the truth.

"Dealing with a man who writes can be very challenging."

"Oh, I'm sure it can," she said with all the enthusiasm of a young woman willing to give it a try.

"Well, get in touch with me if I can be of any help," I concluded weakly.

"I will," she said, the puzzlement obvious in her voice as she wondered why she'd need any help from me, the failed wife.

I put down the phone and felt very guilty at shifting my burden to another, but I simply couldn't carry the load anymore. And even if I could somehow cure Rachel of her ignorance, that would just shift the burden to another anonymous woman who wanted to serve the cause of literature. Twenty years from now when Jonathan had lost his looks, maybe his appeal would wane. Or maybe it would be part of him for his entire life. Either way, he'd leave behind him a line of damaged women who liked to hear him tell stories.

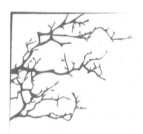

Chapter Twenty-Seven

I pulled up in the jail parking lot three days later and got out of the car. I had a direct line of sight to the nondescript doors that Jonathan was supposed to be leaving from. I leaned back against the car and shivered slightly as the cold November breeze blew through my too-thin jacket. I was nervous. Jonathan had refused to see me or accept my calls ever since he'd accepted Ross Kennedy's version of events that depicted me as a killer who had framed him for the murder of Amanda. I'd half expected him to refuse my offer to pick him up upon his release.

When the door opened right on the stroke of the hour and Jonathan came out, squinting into the bright sunlight, I was surprised at how diminished he looked. Although intellectually I knew that we were of about the same height, in my imagination he had always towered over me. A tall, handsome man whom I was clearly very fortunate to have landed. But the man who finally saw me and headed in the direction of the car, although certainly still handsome, was like a photograph of someone who had once in a bygone age been considered the epitome of male charm. Now there was something faded and outdated about him.

As he drew closer, I walked up to him and put my arms around him and gave him a gentle hug. He stood still but didn't reciprocate. He was carrying a small gym bag.

"Do you get to keep your prison jumpsuit for old time's sake?" I joked.

He didn't crack a smile. Maybe it was too soon for incarceration humor. He threw the bag on the back seat and sat in the front passenger's spot. I got in and began to drive.

"You must be happy to get out," I said. His unnerving silence was driving me into inanities.

"It was horrible in there," he finally said. "And it's all your fault."

"How is it my fault?"

"You killed Amanda and put the blame on me."

"Maggie Boyd killed Amanda, and she tried to kill me."

"Yeah, I heard that's the story that you're telling people."

"It's the truth."

He shook his head hard, his slightly longer than fashionable hair becoming disarrayed.

"It was your jealousy that put me in jail. You couldn't believe that I wouldn't get involved with Amanda, so you killed her and put the blame on me."

"Then how do you explain Maggie's confession."

"She loved me. She really loved me, unlike you. Maggie confessed so they'd have to let me out of jail."

"Maggie was a sociopath. She murdered four people. The police found her husband's body buried in her backyard for God's sake."

"She may have killed her womanizing husband. He deserved it. But you were the one who killed Amanda and Ross."

"And what about Harrison Cole. Did I kill him too? I didn't even know about your involvement with Cole until after he was dead. But Maggie knew, didn't she? You were whining to her all along about how he mistreated you by going back on his word."

Jonathan squirmed slightly in his seat. "She must have done it for me. I told her about Cole going back on his word. I didn't think she'd do anything about it. But Maggie was fiercely loyal, not like you."

"How can you say that? I supported you for years, financially and emotionally."

He gave me a smug smile. "I can intuit things. I know that lately you've been doubting my talent. You've been skeptical that my novel will ever be published, and you only half listen when I talk about writing. It's not obvious, but I know."

I kept my eyes on the road and my face expressionless. I had never suspected that Jonathan could be so perceptive. Even now, it came as something of a surprise to me to look back on how long and gradual had been the decline of my confidence in Jonathan's talent. I had hidden it well even from myself, but apparently not so fully from Jonathan.

I made a turn to head south toward the apartment.

"Where are you going? This isn't the way to our cottage."

"We're not going to the cottage. I've leased an apartment for you close to the college. I've paid in advance for six months. Whether you stay there afterward is up to you. My lawyer will be sending you divorce papers early next week."

"You can't leave me," he said with certainty.

"I am."

"But why?" he asked, suddenly pleading.

"Let's start with your screwing the crazy woman next door."

"That was because you weren't supporting me enough, and I needed help from someone."

"I'm sure you'll find another woman to provide you with that, but it won't be me."

He sat there for a while, a sulky expression on his face.

"I'll make your life miserable. I'll sue you and Lynn for taking the Harrison Cole job away from me."

"You had no contract, Jonathan, there's nothing to sue about. You had your opportunity, and you blew it. If you sue, you'll become known as a troublemaker throughout the publishing industry, and nothing you write will ever be published."

"I never had a chance. You and Lynn stole it away from me."

I pulled up to the curb in front of his apartment house. I reached in my pocket and took out the keys. I tossed them in his lap.

"Your clothes, papers, and laptop are already up there. Everything else will be settled between the lawyers. The place is furnished, but if you want any stuff from the cottage, you can have it. But you better ask soon because it will be going to the dump in a few weeks. Your car is in back in the parking lot. I even left you with a full tank of gas."

He stared down at the keys in his lap. Slowly he took them in his hand.

"You've ruined my life."

"Don't be melodramatic. It's bad writing. Look on the bright side, Rachel Collins is willing to give you three classes next semester. At least she seems happy that you got out of jail."

He opened the door but didn't get out of the car.

"I never got a fair chance to show what I could do. I would have been a great Harrison Cole. You stole that from me."

I'd had enough. "I stole nothing. My writing was better. Lynn told me that your writing was *pedestrian*."

"*Pedestrian*," he repeated slowly, as if it were a foreign word, and he was trying to sound it out for meaning.

He slumped in the seat for a moment as if trying to find the strength to get out of the car. Then he slowly climbed to his feet and shut the car door very gently. He took his bag out of the back without a word and began to drag up the walk to the apartment building. But about halfway up, he straightened his back and a jaunty spring returned to his step. He was probably thinking about Rachel Collins, and how he would have so much to tell her about his evil ex who had snatched literary fame away from him at the last minute. It would make a compelling narrative.

I found myself smiling as I watched the door to the apartment building close behind Jonathan.

He would be fine.

Chapter Twenty-Eight

Eighteen Months Later

I sat in my easy chair directly in front of the television. I was watching the evening news, but not going over history notes. I'd quit my teaching job at the end of the last school year. By that time, the administration was almost pleading with me to stay. The dropping of all charges against Jonathan had left the powers in charge with a guilty feeling regarding their treatment of me. Some of their desire to keep me was the result of a general article in the local newspaper that raised serious questions about the prevalent harassment of teachers by administrators.

I pretended to consider their offer of better pay and more free time, but I never really did. I was tired of being overworked, underpaid, and being treated as if I was of less importance than the janitor. I also found it impossible to forget the quick way in which my many so-called friends had turned against me. There is something about being in a career where you get little respect that causes you to treat others the same way. I looked into the future and didn't like the picture of myself that I saw in twenty years.

Of course, it's easy to be high-minded when you've got an alternative source of income. The first Duke Danforth novel I wrote was very successful, and the second did even better. There was even talk from the publisher that if the third did equally well, they'd like me to begin my own series with a female protagonist. That would mean keeping two plates spinning in the air, but I knew that I was up for it. The idea of creating my own series filled me with anticipation.

The publisher said that I could write both series under the name of Sarah Lane, which had been my legal name for six months since my divorce from Jonathan was finalized. That process was handled completely by the lawyers, and I've never seen Jonathan since the day he got out of my car and walked away.

Lynn says that I will probably be sent on a ten-day book tour around the country in the fall. She warned me that I'll have to learn to play the role of the author. Writers are different from authors, she claimed. A writer knows how terrifically hard it is to put words down on paper, while the author smiles at her fans and gives the impression that it is all a matter of effortless genius. I could draw on my time with Jonathan, the effortless genius, to carry that off.

I appeared on a local television station last week, and the young woman interviewing me asked about my writing process. Did I make an extensive outline before beginning, or did I just fly by the seat of my pants? I told her that I always knew how I wanted the story to end, but I didn't try to anticipate all the steps in between. I let each chapter come to me, and then worked with it to create a narrative that would get my story to where I eventually wanted it to go.

I was going to explain further what I meant, but I could see by the glazed look in her eyes that she'd already heard enough. Television isn't the place for extensive exposition.

The truth is that the approach I take to writing is also the approach I take to life. I know where I want to go, but I accept the events that arise and work with them to get there. For example, I knew from the beginning that Jonathan was having an affair. When clean sheets appeared on the bed one Thursday night, I knew that he was cheating on me. I always changed the sheets on Sunday, and it wasn't in the nature of my housework-adverse husband to make a bed. He wouldn't know how to begin. There had to be a woman involved.

I spent part of that first Thursday night lying in bed sleepless, wondering what I should do. I imagined, of course, that his floozie was some nubile twenty-year-old whom he taught. Jonathan could be quite impressive in the classroom. I never guessed that under her baggy sweats, Maggie was no slouch either. After I learned about Maggie's involvement on the day she tried to kill me, I wondered why she had changed the bed linens, which she'd know would be a sure giveaway of what was going on to any woman. I never had a chance to ask her because of her untimely death, but I can only conclude that she wanted me to know that Jonathan was cheating in the hope that I would divorce him. She must have wondered why I didn't act on my knowledge, and it may have led her to think I was either stupid or weak. A conclusion that later led to her demise.

But it didn't matter to me who the other woman was at the time. What I determined that night is that I wanted to be rid of Jonathan. That posed the problem of how to accomplish it.

I considered divorce at first as being the most common and civilized approach to the matter. The problem with divorce to my mind is that I wasn't convinced that it would rid me of Jonathan once and for all. I could easily imagine him after the divorce, even when involved with another woman or women, turning up on my doorstep, an emotional beggar looking for support. It takes a village of women to raise one male writer, and I no longer wanted to be part of that community. I could, of course, move out of the area, but I didn't see why I should disrupt my life when he was the one cheating.

I flirted with the idea of killing him. However, I knew from television that the spouse is always the first to be suspected, and I wasn't certain my acting abilities would be up to the test. I was also extremely skeptical of the whole concept of the perfect crime, and I certainly had no desire to be rid of Jonathan only to end up in jail myself. I also must admit that I still had a bit of residual affection for Jonathan based on our college days and early years of marriage. It was by now only a faint aftertaste, but it made me reluctant to end his life.

So, I waited. Confident that, just as when I write, a new chapter would come along that would present new creative opportunities to shed my spouse. When I discovered, much to my surprise, that Jonathan was on tap to become the new Harrison Cole, I took heart. If Jonathan finally achieved literary success, he might no longer be in need of my support, and I could happily divorce him, never to be bothered again. When Amanda appeared on the scene, I came up with a double-barreled plan. Perhaps I could get Amanda to seduce him and take him off my hands at the same time as he achieved fame. Those two potent forces together might free me of him.

My show of jealousy in bringing them the apple pie at the hotel room was part of that plan. I knew that Amanda was mainly motivated by the desire to hurt others, particularly women. So, I thought that if I showed my vulnerability, she might set her sights on adding Jonathan to her list of conquests. I had judged Amanda well but underestimated my needy husband. Even Amanda's obvious physical charms didn't blind him to the fact that she was too self-centered to have any energy left to succor him. Amanda had the mothering skills of Medea, and surprisingly, Jonathan detected it and resisted. When he came home from her cottage that night and told me how he had valiantly fended off her advances and at the same time badly damaged his chances at a writing career, I was in despair. Jonathan was going to be an anvil permanently hung around my neck. All I could think to do was to go to Amanda and try to get her to reconsider.

When I walked into the cottage and saw her body sprawled out on the floor, a new possibility occurred to me. It turned out not to be a good one. Looking back, I can only plead that I was in the presence of a newly dead body and under considerable time pressure, but I decided that having Jonathan arrested for Amanda's murder would be a sure way of getting him out of my life. So, after calling the police, I got a plastic tarp from the trunk of my car and carefully removed the bloody fireplace poker lying next to her body. Later that night, I put it under the floor of the trunk of Jonathan's car. I had no way to be sure that the police would ever search his car, but I thought it was a good piece of foreshadowing that might later be developed in the plot.

However, once Jonathan was arrested and I spoke with him in jail, I could immediately see that he would never survive incarceration. Even under the most promising circumstances—let's say he did a plea deal and got only ten years and spent all of it working in the prison library—Jonathan was bound to say something that would leave him bleeding out on the cellblock floor. Jonathan may have had a voice like honey when it came to woman, but to men it came across more like vinegar. I still didn't want Jonathan dead, so now, after putting him in jail, I had to find a way to get him out.

Another repercussion of putting the poker in his trunk is that it drew unwanted attention to me. Ross Kennedy guessed that I had purloined the poker and leaped to the wrong conclusion that it was evidence of my guilt as a murderer. Lieutenant Cranston found it to be an unexplained event that annoyed him and probably would for the rest of his life. But it had one highly positive result. When I mentioned the discovery of the poker in the trunk of Jonathan's car to Maggie, as she was about to put a bullet in my brain, it threw her off stride. Maggie knew that she had left the poker in Cole cottage after she murdered Amanda, and trying to figure out how the poker got into Jonathan's car diverted her attention just long enough for me to make my move. I am convinced that right before she died, she knew that I was the one who had framed her lover.

In any event, I was now left with the problem of getting Jonathan out of jail, while at the same time coming up with a new way of getting rid of him. Once again, I took what life had given me and tried to play it with intelligence and verve. Suddenly, with Jonathan in jail, I had the opportunity to become a writer. I have since found that this is a career for which I am very well suited, but at the time I simply wanted to become Jonathan's worst enemy. I would be the woman who snatched away his chance at a literary career. Even he would never find himself able to come back to me for support if I represented his most bitter disappointment. I must admit that part went swimmingly and resulted in getting Jonathan out of my life. But at the time, I was still left with the question of how to get him out of jail.

Every clue I found and line of investigation I pursued proved futile. And it was only with Maggie arriving as the *deus ex machina* that my bacon was pulled out of the fire. The one person that I had never suspected of harboring any ill will toward me was all the while playing her own long game to get Jonathan for herself. Of course, not to be excessively vain, it was only due to the fact that I had framed Jonathan that Maggie felt forced to reveal herself as a serial killer. But in the end, it was a very close-run thing.

It's never good to have your fate hinge on a piece of torn carpeting.

As I said, I live my life the same way as I write. Whatever cards life deals me, I try to play them with grace and style, attempting to finally achieve the desired result. By that measure, this chapter of my life was a success: Jonathan is gone. Whether he is nestling his needy head in Rachel's muscular bosom or that of some other poor woman is none of my concern. I did send him half of my advance from the first Harrison Cole book, but never got a response. I considered that to be very generous of me. Since I think Jonathan had really kept the money from the first Cole book in his separate bank account to fund a future life with Maggie, I wanted to prove myself to be the bigger person.

An additional result that was delightful as well as unexpected is that I have a new life which offers me infinite opportunities for pleasure and creativity. I frequently smile to myself with satisfaction at what I have accomplished by playing the game well. It's the same satisfaction I feel when I have completed what I think is a good novel.

I turned off the television and got to my feet. I did a little dance in place to get the blood flowing and then stretched languorously, taking an almost sensual pleasure in what was about to come. It was time to go upstairs to my study. It was time to sit in front of my computer and write.

Because that's what writers do.

They write.

Thank you for reading *The Writer's Wife*. I hope you enjoyed it. To see all the books I currently have available, please go to my website at www.glenebisch.com. If you click on the contact page, you can also send me a message or sign up for my newsletter. Feel free to contact me with your comments and suggestions. I will always personally respond. If you enjoyed the book, a review on Amazon is always appreciated, and once again, thanks for taking the time to read *The Writer's Wife*.

Made in the USA
Middletown, DE
15 September 2022

10553395R00126